DOUBLE DATE

By the same author:

DOUBLE WEDDING

WEDDING IN THE FAMILY

SENIOR PROM

THE REAL THING

SHOWBOAT SUMMER

A MAN FOR MARCY

DOUBLE FEATURE

BOY TROUBLE

MARCY CATCHES UP

CLASS RING

WAIT FOR MARCY

PRACTICALLY SEVENTEEN

With Judy du Jardin:

JUNIOR YEAR ABROAD

DOUBLE DATE

by

Rosamond du Jardin

J. B. LIPPINCOTT COMPANY

PHILADELPHIA AND NEW YORK

COPYRIGHT, 1951, 1952, BY ROSAMOND DU JARDIN

PRINTED IN THE UNITED STATES OF AMERICA

TWELFTH IMPRESSION

LIBRARY OF CONGRESS CATALOG CARD NUMBER 52–5102

*To my daughter Judy,
who named this book*

Contents

8 *CONTENTS*

DOUBLE DATE

Chapter One

NEW SCHOOL

*P*ENNY HOWARD loitered self-consciously outside the west entrance of Glen Township High, waiting for her twin sister Pam. Under her arm were several school books and her red corduroy jacket, which had felt so good in the coolness of the September morning seven hours ago. Now the sun slanting across her shoulders was far too warm to permit even the thought of wearing a coat. So Penny clutched it along with her books and tried not to feel awkward and burdened.

Other students streamed past her, girls and boys in laughing, talking, arguing twos and threes and half dozens, none of them paying the slightest attention to Penny. And why should they, she reasoned with herself? None of them knew her, none had laid eyes on her before today. For not only was this the opening day of school for Pam and Penny, it was the first day they had spent at Glen High in their lives. And to start senior year at a new school in a new town where every person and every place seemed strange to you—well, that wasn't a thing to shrug off lightly.

So Penny waited there, wishing Pam would hurry, but knowing darned well she wouldn't, since Pam wasn't the hurrying kind. The soft fall wind swooped at Penny's plaid skirt and she smoothed it down against her knees with her free hand. Then her dark hair was blown forward across her eyes and she had to push it back. A little frown wrinkled its way between her gray eyes. Could she have missed Pam? But that didn't seem possible. They had agreed to meet here after school, surely Pam would have waited.

Penny shifted her books and jacket from one arm to the other. A rather tall girl, with a pixyish face, a dash of freckles, a wide mouth, she might have been attractive laughing and without the anxious frown. But there seemed to be a sort of tenseness, a turned-in-upon-herself air about her that wasn't at all inviting. So the casual glances that touched her flitted by without lingering. And no one spoke.

I might be a statue, Penny thought desolately. I might be something that just grew here, like the ivy climbing up the wall behind me. Come on, Pam. Come on!

Not until Penny had struggled with the wind and her skirt again and shifted her books back and forth a couple more times did Pam finally appear. The heavy door swung out and a masculine hand held it firmly while Pam came through. Penny was so relieved to see her twin, she didn't notice at first that Pam wasn't alone.

"I thought you'd never get here!" she exclaimed.

"Am I awfully late?" Pam asked apologetically. "I'm sorry—but I actually got lost. It's a big school."

Looking into Pam's face was like holding a mirror up to Penny's. They were so much alike. Except that Pam's wide mouth was curved in an enchanting smile and there was no frown between her gray eyes. The wind wouldn't dare whip Pam's plaid skirt awkwardly above her knees. It simply molded it against her in a very flattering way.

And Pam's arms were free and unburdened. She wore her red jacket slung jauntily over her shoulders and in one hand she carried a single text book. Belatedly Penny realized that the dark-haired boy who had held the door open and the tall practically white-haired boy who had emerged right behind Pam were not casual passers-by, but were with her sister.

"If you hadn't sighted a couple of familiar faces from math class, you might have wandered around school all night." The dark-haired boy's eyes narrowed a little in laughter behind his shell-rimmed glasses.

"That's right," Pam laughed back at him in her most beguiling way. "Thanks for rescuing me, you two."

"Any time," the platinum-blond boy chuckled. "We're in training to replace those St. Bernards they send around the Alps with brandy kegs hung on 'em."

Penny laughed at that, too. And the sound of her laughter seemed to remind Pam once more of her presence. "Penny," she said, indicating the blond boy with just a touch of light fingers on his forearm, "this is Mike Bradley. And this is Randy—Patterson, is it?" She glanced at the dark-haired boy questioningly.

"You're close," he assured her. "It's Kirkpatrick."

"Sorry," Pam said in her easy, casual way that Penny would have given almost anything to be able to duplicate. "This is my sister, Penny."

"Hi, Penny," Mike grinned at her.

"How do you do," Randy Kirkpatrick's acknowledgment of the introduction was a shade more formal, but his smile was as warm.

"How do you do," Penny murmured. And immediately she wished she'd said, "Hi." Still, if she had said "Hi," that wouldn't have seemed quite right to her, either. She felt herself caught up in a familiar and hated embarrassment and hoped she wasn't coloring. If only she had half Pam's poise and self-assurance!

"Never would have suspected you two were related," Mike said, straight-faced.

Randy Kirkpatrick looked from Pam to Penny and back again a couple of times. "It's just like seeing double."

"Now where have we heard that before?" Pam asked Penny. But she didn't wait for an answer. Instead she tucked her hand through her sister's arm and smiled impartially from one boy to the other. "We have to be getting home now."

"Which way do you go?" Mike Bradley asked.

And Randy said, "My heap's parked around back. Glad to give you girls a lift."

"It's not far—" Penny began.

But the slight pressure of Pam's hand on her arm stopped her. And Pam's voice poured over hers, smooth as cream, saying, "It's just down on Main Street, but if you don't mind short trips, we'd love a lift, wouldn't we, Penny?"

"Why—yes," Penny murmured.

The four of them descended the long flight of stone steps. Glen High perched on a hilltop, its steep front campus sloping down to the street. Behind the school and on a lower level were the athletic field, with seats in tiers at either end, and a parking space for student and faculty cars. Beyond the parking space and athletic field a small lake glimmered blue in the bright fall sunshine, with the well-tended lawns and shrubbery and tall old trees of the town park surrounding it.

"I love the lake," Pam said with her usual bubbling enthusiasm. "Imagine a school with a lake right behind it! Why, the school we went to in Chicago had no campus at all. You came down the steps and there you were right on a busy city street, with buses zooming past and a traffic cop at the corner."

At least, Penny thought, feeling a touch of nostalgia for their old school, it was all perfectly familiar. There she had known where she was going, where everything was. She had had friends. But she'd get acquainted here eventually, she reminded herself. It wouldn't always seem so strange.

"No foolin'?" Mike Bradley said. "I don't think I'd like that. I'm strictly a small-town guy myself."

He looked, Penny reflected, like a Viking, with his fair hair, his blue eyes, his broad-shouldered rangy height. Her heart quickened as he caught her eyes on his face and grinned at her.

Then his attention shifted back to Pam, who was chattering on easily. "It's so wonderful out here in Glenhurst. I just love the suburbs. And we'll like it even better when we've had time to really make friends. Everyone seems so nice and easy to get acquainted with, I know it won't take long."

"It's a pretty friendly town," Randy Kirkpatrick agreed, smiling at Pam, obviously charmed by the warmth of her personality. He asked then, "How long have you lived out here?"

"Oh, just a teensy while," Pam said, her gray eyes wide on his. "Only a few weeks. And you know how it is when you move. We've been so terribly rushed and busy trying to get settled and all—well, we just haven't had a chance to meet anyone, really. Now that school's started it'll be different, though."

It would be different for Pam at any rate, Penny thought a trifle ruefully. How could twin sisters, who looked so much alike that most people couldn't tell them apart, be so unlike inside? She had pondered the question many times before and found no answer. How could Pam chatter on so animatedly, so effortlessly, keeping these boys she scarcely knew interested and amused, instilling in them a desire to get better acquainted? Penny could think of nothing at all to add to Pam's running comments. Beside her sister she felt leaden and dull and miserably aware of the poor impression she was making. Trudging along with the others, Penny spoke only when spoken to directly. Casual, friendly talk eddied about her like a warm current, while she contributed little more than monosyllables. Not that the others seemed to notice. Pam's voice filled any void that might otherwise have been left by Penny's silence.

When Randy stopped beside a light green convertible in the graveled parking space, Pam's eyes widened in appreciation. "This is yours?" she asked. "This is the heap you mentioned?"

"Only its outside looks good," Randy grinned modestly.

"Don't let him kid you," Mike drawled. "He's filthy rich and this is just one of the little baubles his doting family lavishes on him. Now me, I'm the poor-but-honest type. Any car I get I got to pay for. So, I walk, only when I get offered a ride."

"If you don't shut your big mouth in a hurry," Randy said good-humoredly, "you'll walk right now."

"Sorry," Mike said. "I take every word of it back. Actually, girls, he only rides to school because the Kirkpatrick hovel is a couple of miles away. And he only takes me home because I happen to live on his usual route. And he only takes you home—" he broke off to regard Randy quizzically. "Just why is it you're taking these two gorgeous tomatoes home, chum?"

Randy laid his hand lightly on Pam's shoulder, a teasing gleam in his dark glance. "I'm afraid she'll get lost again."

"I suppose I'll never live that down," Pam laughed. "It's those three floors at the back of the school and only two in front that confused me."

"We know," Mike soothed. "They should supply guides for new students. Suggest it at the next Council meeting, Randy."

"Will do," Randy said.

They all clambered into the green car then, Penny and Mike in the small back seat that obviously cramped Mike's long legs, Pam and Randy in front.

"Where to on Main Street?" Randy asked, angling the car adeptly out of the parking space.

"Just across from the post office," Pam said. "Second house from the corner."

"Say," Mike exclaimed, "that's the old Crandall place! Do you live there?"

Pam nodded, smiling at him across her shoulder.

"But isn't it fixed over into some kind of a shop?"

"The downstairs is," Pam informed him. We live up. And it isn't *some* kind of a shop, I'll have you know," she added with mock indignation. "It's 'Howard House—Interior Decoration.' We just haven't got our sign out in front yet."

"You mean your father's an interior decorator?" Randy asked interestedly.

Penny's throat felt a little chokey, as it always seemed

to when anyone spoke of her father. And Pam's face was momentarily grave, saying, "Not our father—he's dead. Mother's the interior decorator. She worked in a big Chicago shop for years. But just this summer she happened to stumble on the Crandall place and saw right away what a wonderful set-up it would be for a shop of her own. So, she bought it and we've all been working like crazy to fix it up."

"You've certainly done wonders with the outside," Mike said. "The place was a wreck. And being so close to the business district, no one would buy it to live in."

Pam nodded, smiling again. "That's how we could afford it," she confided. "And if you think the outside's improved, you should see the inside. Mother's so clever, she has such terrific ideas. Like that picture window facing the street—it's practically a show window and yet it doesn't spoil the looks of the house."

"Yeah," Mike said, "I've noticed that."

And Randy added, "A shop like that should do a good business in Glenhurst. There's nothing at all like it around."

"I know," Pam nodded. "Mother investigated that angle first of all. She figured, with a really good shop right here in the community, there'd be no point in people having to go all the way in to the city for furnishings and ideas. It's the ideas that are most important—and Mother has such wonderful ones. . . ."

The way Pam made Howard House sound all established and successful, instead of shaky and barely started and operating on a shoestring, aroused Penny's profound admiration. Pam was so wonderfully assured about everything, never bumbling around at a loss for words, always able to make anything sound like a gay adventure. And it wasn't that she boasted or exaggerated, either. She was simply able to put the best face possible on things, to stress the good aspects and tone down the bad ones.

Penny sighed, a very small sigh that none of the others noticed. It wasn't that she envied her sister—not really. She only wished she could be like her in other ways than their surface physical resemblance. Listening to Pam run on, so effortlessly, so interestingly, Penny thought it was no wonder everyone liked her, liked to be with her. Nor was it any wonder that Penny's own uncertainties and inadequacies showed up so glaringly by comparison.

Chapter Two

CARBON COPY

WHEN Richard Howard was killed in his skidding car on an icy stretch of road, his wife, Celia, had to pick up the broken pieces of her life and weld them together as best she could. She loved Rick deeply, but she was a valiant, forward-looking person. And there were her ten-year-old daughters to consider and all the responsibilities attendant on their upbringing.

It had been necessary for Celia to get a job, so that Rick's modest insurance might be kept as a backlog of security. So Celia's widowed mother, whom the twins called Gran, came up from a small Indiana town to live with them in their Chicago apartment and take care of Pam and Penny. Gran didn't like the city too well, but she made the best of it. She was a brisk, energetic woman, with a sense of humor that was dry and unfailing. Gran's hair was white and her figure comfortably cushioned, but not fat. Her bright blue eyes didn't miss much that was going on. She was aware that times had changed since she was a girl, but, unlike many grandmothers, she felt that some of the changes might possibly be for the better. She and the twins were fond of each other, they got along fine. And even when Penny and Pam reached their teens, they found Gran understanding and not too hopelessly old-fashioned. It would have been wonderful if Mother could stay at home all the time. But, since she couldn't, Gran made a pretty good substitute.

Celia herself regretted that her job left her so little time to spend with the girls. This was especially true as they grew up and Gran confessed privately that she felt her age was against her in coping with a couple of modern teenagers.

"It wasn't too much for me," Gran admitted to Celia, "when their problems were mainly skinned knees and school grades and checking up on whether they'd washed behind their ears. But now that boys and lipstick and how late to stay out on dates are the vital issues—well, I don't know, Cele, whether I'm up to handling them or not." She sighed, adding, "And this business lately of Pam being more popular than Penny—that's just a little ticklish."

"I know," Celia said, laying an affectionate hand on her mother's shoulder, "but it would be ticklish for anyone. Twins are a problem sometimes. And raising them in a city apartment isn't the best set-up, either. But you handle things as well as anyone could. I only wish I could be around more to help you. . . ."

Celia had a dream, shared only with the twins and Gran, of opening an interior decorating shop of her own, somewhere in the suburbs, perhaps, where they could live close by and she could arrange her working hours according to a more elastic schedule. But the idea remained nothing more than a wistful daydream for quite a long time.

Then one early spring night Celia came home from work practically popping with excitement. She was a slim, pretty woman whose light brown hair showed only a touch of gray and whose blue eyes were bright and direct like Gran's. They were even brighter than usual now. And scarcely did Celia have her hat and coat off than she was demanding, "What are we having for dinner? Can it possibly wait? Because we've just got to have a family conference!"

"Casserole," Gran said. "I'll turn off the oven right away and it'll be all right anytime."

Penny had been intent on her homework, curled up on the couch, surrounded by books. Pam had been lying in front of the record-player, dreamily listening to Perry Como. Now she switched him off in mid-song and both she and Penny regarded their mother expectantly. Family conferences weren't usually called so decisively unless some vital matter was at stake.

As soon as Gran had bustled back from the kitchen, Celia began to speak. She didn't sit down, although her feet were usually pretty tired by evening, and she clasped her hands together in an entreating sort of way. She said solemnly, "Now we must consider this question rationally. It's not a thing to decide without thought. I want us all to be happy over whatever decision we come to and convinced absolutely that it's the right thing to do."

All of them stared at her, surprised at her unusual seriousness. Then Penny's eyes slipped away to meet Pam's and an unspoken question flashed between them. Could Mother want to remarry? It was not too remote a possibility. There was Harry Morton at the store where she worked. He had taken Mother out quite a bit and sent her roses on her birthday. Neither of the twins thought much of Harry Morton, with his thin hair and thick waistline. Surely Mother wouldn't get this excited over a proposal from him!

Penny felt her breath puff out in a little sigh of relief

as Mother continued, "I was 'way out in the suburbs today in a town called Glenhurst. It was the final check-up on that Currier job we've been so busy with at the store. And as I walked back to the train, I just happened to see this house . . ."

As Mother's voice went on, warmly intent and enthusiastic, Penny seemed to see it, too. Drab and gray with the ravages of time, a square old house of two stories, set rather close to the street. And yet, according to Mother, run-down and neglected and practically overgrown with rank shrubbery though it was, there was still a square solidity about it that indicated strong foundations and fine workmanship.

"A FOR SALE sign was half-hidden in the weeds," Mother explained, "all weathered, as though it had been there a long time. At first I couldn't understand why no one had seen the house's wonderful possibilities for remodeling. And then it struck me—the trouble was the location. It's right in the business section, really. There's a post office and stores in the same block. That would be a big disadvantage if a person were merely looking for a place to live—but—well," Mother chuckled suddenly in an enchanting way she had, like a child who has been caught in mischief, "I had half an hour to kill till train time, so I couldn't resist stopping at the real estate office to ask a few questions. That," she informed them, "was when I met Mr. Hancock, Mr. Lucius Hancock, quite the most terrific salesman I ever encountered in my life!"

"High-pressure?" Gran asked.

"Low-pressure," Mother corrected. "No one ever *undersold* anything so completely. First of all, I asked the price and it was quite reasonable. But as soon as I mentioned the fact that I thought it would make a good location for an interior decorating business, he drew his beetling brows together and began pointing out drawbacks to me so fast it made my head spin."

"He doesn't sound much like a real estate man," Pam said.

"Darlings," Mother told them all, "he doesn't look like one, either. He's quite old and he has beautiful thick snow-white hair and these rather overwhelming eyebrows—" she broke off, obviously struck by a sudden thought. "He looks like Santa Claus, only without the whiskers, and if you can imagine Santa in slacks and a jacket and quite a dazzling sport shirt."

Pam and Penny giggled at the picture thus summoned up. But Mother informed them, "He's rather a dear when you get used to him. Anyway," she went on, "we argued for a while and then I realized that he thought I meant the house should be torn down and a business building erected to be used for a decorating shop. When I finally made it clear to him that what I was talking about was a shop on the first floor of the old house and living quarters above—well, he turned very co-operative. He'd been against the idea at first because he couldn't bear the thought of the house being demolished. He says the place is a sort of landmark in the town and there are all too few of them left. Of course, I didn't commit myself—I wouldn't without discussing the idea with all of you and having you see the place and give your opinions." Celia's shining eyes swept from Gran to Pam to Penny and she said, "I think you'll all love the town. And the house could be fixed up without a lot of money. Mr. Hancock and I looked it over very carefully—I was an hour late getting back to the store. But if we could work it out and swing the mortgage and repairs without using all Rick's insurance—well, it's exactly the sort of set-up I've dreamed of. I'd be right there in the house with you from morning till night, except when I was out on jobs. I could see so much more of you and be of more help. . . ."

The idea appealed to the twins as much as it did to Gran, all of them caught fire from Celia's enthusiasm. They went out to Glenhurst the following Sunday, saw the house and fell in love with it, met Mr. Hancock and were charmed with his friendliness, his desire to help. Not that they rushed ahead blindly. Celia talked over her plans with friends in the same business, checked with wholesale furniture dealers, all sorts of sources of supply. Finally there seemed no further reason for delay, so the house was bought, Celia gave up her job and the four of them moved to Glenhurst.

The house had been painted and its crumbling fieldstone chimney repaired before they moved into it. But much work remained to be done on the interior. Celia had a man highly recommended by Lucius Hancock do the papering and painting. But she and the twins and even Gran were endlessly busy, polishing and cleaning and furbishing, making the upper rooms bloom into liveability, the lower ones take on the aspects of a smart decorator's shop. Celia was so clever, so original. She had such a way of combining furniture and fabrics effectively. People began coming to Howard House long before the family was truly settled, or the shop finally arranged.

"I think it's going to work out," Celia told Gran. "It'll take time, of course, to get firmly established. I don't mean it'll be easy. But I have a hunch we didn't make any mistake when we came to Glenhurst."

Celia often had hunches and sometimes they worked out. The twins and Gran hoped this was one of her more successful ones. Because all of them liked Glenhurst and wanted to stay there forever.

One day in their bedroom Pam told Penny, "I can't wait till school starts, can you? I can't wait till we have a whole new crowd of friends and all sorts of different places to go and things to do. I can't wait!"

Penny felt a surge of the same impatience that was nipping at Pam. But aloud she said calmly, "I can wait."

Pam jumped up and swung around the room in a slow dreamy waltz, her eyes closed, her face lifted to an imaginary partner. "We don't even know what the names of their dances at Glen High will be, or who'll take us—or anything!"

Penny said, "So long as somebody takes us." She said it in a joking sort of way, but there was a grain of seriousness underneath, sharp and troubling as a cinder in your eye. Penny was never quite sure of being asked to dances, unless Pam fixed it up for her, unless Pam said airily to her date, "Bring along someone nice for Penny, will you? It'll be more fun double-dating." Pam was very generous about that sort of thing, still Penny would have liked it better for some boy to ask her for a date, totally irrespective of her sister.

But Pam said confidently, "We'll get asked, never fear."

Pam had every reason for confidence. Penny thought, a feeling of hope lifting her spirits, maybe it'll be different out here in Glenhurst. Maybe someone will pay some attention to me as an individual, not just put up with me because I'm Pam's sister. Maybe there'll be a boy who'll like me, personally . . .

She hadn't gone so far as to imagine just how he'd look. If she had, Penny thought, riding home from school in the back seat of Randy Kirkpatrick's green convertible, he might well have been a reasonable facsimile of Mike Bradley. But was Mike paying any attention to her? Was she dazzling him with her charms? Would he by any stretch of the imagination ask her for a date, rather than Pam? The answer to all these questions, Penny knew, was a flat "no." For Mike Bradley was leaning forward to listen to Pam; he was giving her the greater share of his attention, just as Randy Kirkpatrick in the front seat was.

It was always like this, Penny thought desolately. It always would be. She stopped trying to think of something to say, something witty and arresting that would catch Mike's wandering attention. She wrapped herself in her familiar shell of not caring, or, at least, of pretending not to care. Sometimes she pretended so well she had herself fooled. But not today. Not quite.

Penny's throat ached with the knowledge that things weren't going to be different for her at Glen High after all. It was going to be the same old routine of following after Pam, of trying to keep up with her and imitate her winning ways.

"Just call me Carbon Copy," Penny thought, her lips twisting a little in a wry smile. But no one was looking at her, so no one noticed.

Chapter Three

PAM'S TECHNIQUE

*W*HEN Penny came into the wide, gray-carpeted entrance hall, she saw that Mother was busy with two well-dressed feminine customers. They were standing in what had once been a living room, but was now the main salesroom of Howard House. Mother's gray suit with the little lime scarf at the throat went beautifully with the greens and grays and bright tangerine tones of the salesroom. Mother always dressed to match her surroundings, she was so clever about details like that.

She smiled at Penny and said, "Hello, dear," then went on with a spirited discussion of the comparative merits of several bolts of drapery material which the two customers seemed to be considering.

Penny turned back for one quick look through the glass of the door to see whether Pam was coming. But Pam was leaning her elbows on the door of the convertible, laughing gayly with Mike and Randy, both of whom now occupied the front seat. Penny could have lingered, too, if she had liked, but there had seemed no point in it. None of the others had been paying any attention to her.

She made her way slowly up the stairs. Here in the small apartment where the twins and their mother and grandmother lived, the furnishings were tasteful, but far from new. The colors in the chintz drapes were sun-muted, the rugs showed signs of wear, everything had a comfortable lived-in look. Personally Penny liked the easy informality of these rooms much better than the smart perfection of the lower floor, which all the customers exclaimed over. But, of course, none of the customers saw the upper rooms.

Gran was sitting in the cheerful living room, the irregular shape of which was due to the fact that a partition had been removed and two former bedrooms thrown together. Gran was knitting, which she almost always did whenever she sat down. She found knitting a form of relaxation, since she had done so much of it she didn't have to look at what she was doing. She could knit and talk, or listen to the radio, or even read. It was wonderful for Pam and Penny, who never ran out of hand-knit sweaters.

Now a shaft of sunlight gleamed on Gran's crisply curly white hair. When she noticed Penny, she smiled and said, "Well, hello. I didn't hear you come upstairs. How did it go?"

Penny knew Gran meant the first day of school, not the encounter with two very attractive new boys. Gran wouldn't know anything about that, unless she'd been looking out the window.

"Okay," Penny said. "Sort of strange, of course."

"That won't last long," Gran said confidently.

Penny put her books and jacket down on the arm of the couch. No sound disturbed the stillness but the brisk click of Gran's flying needles, the faint murmur of Mother's and the customers' voices from downstairs.

"Homework already?" Gran frowned at the stack of books. "Aren't they loading it on a bit early? First day of school!"

"There's not too much of it," Penny said.

"I'll bet Pam didn't bring any home," Gran chuckled.

"Just one book," Penny admitted with a smile.

"She figures she'll use yours if she needs 'em," Gran said. "It'd be a good joke on her if you didn't bring a book home some night."

"I don't mind," Penny said. As always, she found herself impelled to defend Pam. "It wouldn't make much sense for both of us to drag the same books home."

Gran smiled at Penny, her blue eyes crinkling at the corners, seeming to see deep down inside her. But Penny didn't mind that, either. She and Gran understood each other pretty well.

"Tell me how things went," Gran said. "How was the new school and all?"

Penny began dutifully, "It's quite a big school, even bigger than it seems from the outside. There are two floors in front and three in the back, because of its being on a hill. The teachers seem okay—of course, I don't know them all yet, but the ones I've met are nice."

She knew that Pam could describe it all much more interestingly. Pam's words would come so fast they would trip over each other, telling about the school, the teachers, adding funny little anecdotes. Pam could make such a wonderful story out of practically anything, while even unusual things that happened to Penny seemed to come out quite dull and ordinary in the telling.

Gran asked, "Where is Pam? Didn't she come home with you?"

Penny nodded. "A couple of very smooth fellows brought us home. Pam's still out in front talking to them.

One has a convertible. His name's Kirkpatrick. The other one's Mike Bradley."

Penny liked the shape of his name on her lips. She thought of his rangy height and his eyes that were so blue and so disconcertingly direct. She remembered the engaging way he grinned and that astonishingly blond hair of his. She hoped hard that Pam would like Randy Kirkpatrick best, but she was afraid to count on it, even though Randy was very nice-looking, too, besides owning the convertible.

Anyway, Penny reflected with a little sigh, it probably wouldn't make any difference which one Pam preferred. Even if it were Randy, Mike wasn't likely to waste much time on Pam's quiet sister. He had hardly spoken to her all the way home. Both boys had had eyes only for Pam. Penny should be used to that by this time.

Gran said, "Well, for pity's sake, why didn't you say so sooner?" She got up with alacrity and went over to the window to look out unobtrusively. Penny couldn't resist the temptation to follow and peek over Gran's plump shoulder. "They're just going," Gran said. "That's quite a car for a high-school boy to have."

Penny turned away from the window quickly as she heard the front door open. By the time Pam reached the living room, Penny was hanging up her jacket in the bedroom closet.

"Hi, sweetie-pie," Pam addressed Gran. "Did you see those two perfectly swoony new males? They're in my math class—lucky me! The dark one's Randy and the blond one's Mike. Randy's sort of quiet, but cute, and the car is his very own. His parents gave it to him over a year ago on his sixteenth birthday. Mike's got a perfectly terrific personality. And that hair! Do you know what he does to it?" Pam asked, laughing, then rushed on, not waiting for an answer, "He uses peroxide and ammonia on it every now and then, just for kicks. He's so crazy!"

"He must be," Gran said. "I never heard of such nonsense!"

"Oh, he's blond, anyway," Pam said. "But not quite that blond. He says white hair is so distinguished, the teachers have to treat him with respect. He's really awfully cute. But so is Randy—" she broke off to ask, "Where's Penny? Didn't she come up yet?"

"She went thataway," Gran said, in the best tradition of Western movies.

"Penny?" Pam called, coming into the bedroom, where her twin was brushing her hair at the plaid-gingham-skirted dressing table. "Oh, there you are! Why did you fade away like that? Didn't you like Mike and Randy?"

Penny's eyes met her sister's in the mirror. Didn't Pam really know why she had left? Couldn't she sense how it felt to be in a gay, laughing group and yet not really a part of it? Aloud she said merely, "I told you I was going in, but nobody seemed to hear me"

Pam asked again, "But didn't you like them, Penny?"

"Of course," Penny admitted. "They both seem awfully nice and lots of fun—especially Mike. But—well, it's pretty clear who they're interested in."

Pam chuckled, a low, throaty sound that was singularly pleasing. "Oh, I don't know," she said. "Neither of them paid much attention to me this morning in Math. It wasn't until I saw them in the corridor after school and had the brilliant idea of pretending to be lost—"

Penny stared at her in surprise. "You mean you weren't?"

"Of course not," Pam said smugly. "It was just a way of impressing myself on their consciousness. Showing me the way to the entrance made them feel big and male and helpful—and all the rest followed as a matter of course"

Penny shook her head wonderingly. "How do you know things like that? They never even occur to me."

"Oh," Pam said airily, "it's just a little something I picked up around the time I was in seventh grade, I think."

"I didn't pick it up," Penny said. Her glance at Pam was filled with admiration. "Why, if I tried to pretend I was lost when I really wasn't—it would show! I mean, I'd blush or do something to give it away. I'd never get away with it."

Pam patted her shoulder affectionately. "You're too honest," she said. "Honesty is all right in its place, but in dealing with boys you have to be a little flexible. Now look at today, for instance. Just by pretending to be dumb and helpless, I got us a ride home from school in the swoony convertible. And we got acquainted with two of the cutest boys I've seen around. You have to take advantage of opportunities like that."

Penny said slowly, "Yes, I guess so."

But she knew she couldn't ever do it. Not with the finesse Pam used so effortlessly.

Pam fluffed her dark hair out around her head with the brush, then gave it a little shake, like a wet cocker spaniel. Each curl and wave assumed its proper place with wonderful precision. "You know what?" Pam said. "I think we ought to make a point of dressing just alike, at least for the next few weeks. That way, we'll make more of a splash at school. After all, being twins gives us a certain distinction and we might as well make the most of it."

There Pam went, Penny thought, managing their everyday life like some sort of showman, shrewdly playing up their assets and toning down their liabilities.

"Right at first," Pam said, "I think we ought to build ourselves up in every way we can, so people will notice us and realize we're around. Okay with you?"

"I suppose so," Penny agreed. As always, she found it hard to stand out against any of Pam's ideas. They always sounded so plausible and Pam, she knew, was capable of carrying them out with all the canny, strategical shrewdness of a general planning a big battle. If only she, Penny, had a little more flair for such things. At any rate, she could try.

Pam climbed out of her plaid skirt and sweater and into an old white shirt and blue jeans. Penny put on her old clothes, too. After a long silence, Pam said dreamily, "I wonder which one will call up first?"

"Randy or Mike, you mean?" There was a trace of wistful envy in Penny's voice for Pam's self-confidence.

"Natch," Pam said. "I'll bet it'll be Randy."

Penny's heart beat just a little faster. Did that mean Pam hoped it would be Randy? "Why?" she asked aloud.

"Oh, he's more impressionable, I imagine," Pam said. "Mike seems like the rugged type—holds out just to prove to himself he can hold out. But that kind melts fast once they start." She chuckled. There was a gleam Penny didn't like too well in her eye and a little confident smile played about her mouth. "You want to make a small bet?"

"What kind of a bet?" Penny asked suspiciously.

"I'll bet you," Pam elaborated, "a pair of *very* sheer

Nylons that one of those boys calls up or comes over within the next hour."

Penny's eyes widened just a little. This was super-confidence, even for Pam. Still she shook her head decisively. "I won't bet. My budget's already limping."

"You're smart," Pam said. "It was worth a try anyhow. I could use some new stockings."

"How can you be so sure?" Penny asked wonderingly. "Why, for all we know, both Randy and Mike may have steady girls."

"Maybe yes," Pam said airily, "maybe no."

"Did—anything they said point one way or the other?" Penny's tone was a shade more anxious than she realized.

Pam smiled at her. "Why, baby, I believe you *are* interested. Which one?"

"I told you," Penny said, coloring just a little and hating it, "I thought they were both awfully nice."

Pam nodded judiciously. "That's right, don't go making up your mind in too big a hurry." She went on then to answer Penny's question. "No, neither of them said anything about having a regular girl or not having one. There's just a kind of gleam in their eyes that usually indicates a free man."

Penny hoped she was right, especially about Mike. "But just because they are free—*if* they are," she said slowly, "I still don't see how you can be so positive one of them will call up tonight."

Pam laughed then, her warm contagious laugh that you couldn't hold out against, that made you join in even if you were pretty sure she was laughing at you. "Baby, you're so dense sometimes," she said, giving Penny an affectionate little hug. "It's really elemental. I left my math book in the car."

"Pam!" Penny exclaimed. "You didn't!"

"Um-hum," Pam admitted blandly. "So naturally one or the other of them will discover it and not want me to be worried—"

The sound of the phone ringing cut her off. Penny only kept her ear cocked long enough to learn that it was Randy Kirkpatrick calling. With a little inner glow of relief, she started in on her homework. A few minutes later, after telling Gran all about it, Pam came beamingly back to the bedroom. "Randy's going to bring my book back tonight," she said. "I told him I wouldn't need it till after dinner."

"I don't suppose you told him you could use mine and get along without yours entirely?" Penny asked drily.

"Naturally not!" Pam chuckled.

"Honestly, Pam," Penny shook her head, "I don't see how you can pull a trick like that! Aren't you afraid he'll suspect you did it on purpose?"

Pam shrugged and went over to study her reflection appraisingly in the mirror. "I don't care if he does suspect. Even so, it only indicates I'm interested in him enough to want him to come over. Of course, it might have been a teensy bit nicer if Mike had found my book—he's such fun. But Randy's cute, too."

Penny stared at Pam's back for a long minute before bringing her attention back to her English assignment. She could never learn to be like her sister, not really, not if she lived a thousand years.

Chapter Four

ESCAPE TO THE LIBRARY

*G*RAN had dinner almost ready and Pam, whose turn it happened to be, had set the table in the little dining alcove, when Mother came upstairs. Mother kicked off her shoes, as was her habit, and dropped down wearily on the couch beside Penny.

"I'm tired," she admitted, running her fingers back through her short gray-blond hair. "This has been quite a day! I wish every one was this good."

"Lots of business?" Penny asked.

Mother nodded. "Oh, some of the sales were small, but people kept coming in all day. Those two women who were here when you got home bought some very expensive drapery material to be made up. And this morning I sold a pair of loveseats. I do hope Mr. Hancock can get me that old station wagon he said he had a line on. It would be wonderful for deliveries and carting stuff around."

Pam came bursting in from the kitchen then to give Mother a big hug and announce that dinner was ready. Without stopping for breath, she was off on a marathon description of the new school, the teachers, the events of the day. As Penny had been sure she would, Pam climaxed her recital with her meeting with Mike and Randy and the lift home she and Penny had been given. By the time Pam had reached the point of having left her Math book in the car, they were halfway through Gran's excellent dinner.

"So Randy's bringing it back," Pam smiled knowingly at Mother, "tonight."

Mother smiled, too. "I'm glad I'll get a chance to meet him."

Gran said drily, "In my day we left a glove or a handkerchief where it would do the most good. Now it's a book."

"I'll bet you left a lot of them, too," Pam teased. "You're still a flirt."

"Don't be silly." Obviously, though, Gran wasn't displeased. There was an amused sparkle in her blue eyes.

"That's all right," Pam insisted with mock disapproval. "Look at the way Mr. Hancock's always dropping by to see if there isn't anything he can do for us."

"Lucius Hancock's a real estate agent," Gran said. "It's his business to be nice to people who buy houses from him. Don't go implying you inherit your flibbertigibbet ways from me, young lady."

"It must be Mother, then," Pam said.

Penny felt her mother's amused, questioning glance stray from Pam to her. "Did you think these boys were nice, too, Penny? Or is Pam getting carried away in her usual exuberant manner?"

"Oh, they are nice," Penny admitted. "Randy's sort of quiet, but not dull or anything. And Mike's lots of fun."

"I think he's the hard-to-get type," Pam elaborated. "You know, the sort of personality that resists letting a woman wrap him around her little finger?"

"You mean you may have to work a bit harder on him?" Gran chuckled.

"You see?" Pam appealed to Mother. "I told you she was a flirt. She knows all the angles!"

Dinner was gay and leavened with laughter. It was Penny's turn to do the dishes, so she wouldn't let them linger too long at the table. Penny always wanted to get unpleasant duties out of the way as quickly as possible. Pam's technique was just the opposite. "Never do today what you can put off till tomorrow," was her motto. But Penny preferred to following the saying in its true form.

This evening she had a special reason for wanting to get through with her work quickly. She planned to be out of the house before Randy Kirkpatrick arrived. It wasn't that she didn't like him. It was simply that she felt such a fifth wheel to be hanging around when a boy came to see Pam. Randy would be put in the unhappy position of having to spread his attentions between the two of them. If he wanted to ask Pam to go for a ride, or out for a bite to eat, as he very well might, there was Penny squarely in the way. Either she must be left rudely at home, or asked, not too willingly, to accompany them. Penny had been put on that uncomfortable spot before. She had made up her mind just how to escape it this time.

So hardly was the last dish dried and put away, than Penny was gathering up her jacket and loose-leaf notebook and announcing, "I've got to go over to the library for a while. We're studying Elizabethan drama in English and it'll take some research."

The public library was only a short distance away, no problem at all to get to. And Penny's need to do some research on Elizabethan drama was valid enough—it was just that there wasn't nearly as big a rush about it as her manner implied. But neither Gran nor Mother knew that. And Pam was in the bedroom changing her clothes again, so she wasn't even aware that Penny was leaving. Not, Penny thought, that Pam necessarily would have tried to stop her. Pam was a realist. She, too, knew that their being twins sometimes posed a problem for the boys.

Penny ran lightly down the stairs and let herself out into the crisply cool darkness of early evening. The breeze smelled good, moist and clean and with just a faint edge of wood smoke, as if someone near by had been burning brush. Down the hill, the main business section of Glenhurst lay spread out, multicolored lights twinkling from the stores' signs and windows, giving it a bustling festive air. Penny loved this view of the village and she walked slowly along toward the library, giving herself an extra minute or two to enjoy it.

Climbing the broad stone steps of the compact red brick building, Penny permitted herself an extravagantly improbable daydream. Wouldn't it be wonderful if she would open the heavy door, get the book she needed and carry it over to the table in the corner, only to discover that Mike Bradley was already sitting there? Penny could just see him, his blond hair gleaming under the light, looking up and recognizing her with his quick easy smile.

She could just hear him saying, "Well, what do you know? If it isn't Penny Howard. Don't tell me you're checking up on Elizabethan drama, too."

And she would say, smiling, too, not feeling a bit ill at ease or self-conscious, "I certainly am. You didn't think you had a monopoly on it, did you?"

And Mike would answer, indicating the chair beside him,

maybe even going so far as to get up and pull it out for her, "Well, sit right down and we'll work on this together. Shall we start with Hamlet?"

"Oh, yes," Penny would answer, sitting down and looking up at Mike gravely. "Hamlet's one of my very favorites!"

And by the strangest coincidence, Hamlet would be one of Mike Bradley's favorites, too. And they would read part of it together, their heads very close over the open book, their shoulders touching. Maybe, if the library was practically deserted, as it sometimes was, Mike would read the soliloquy aloud. His voice would be low, but rich and deep with meaning, the way Laurence Olivier's voice had sounded in the movie version, which Penny had enjoyed so much she saw it three times. Especially that part that went: "To die, to sleep; To sleep: perchance to dream!" She could just hear Mike saying that. And they would proceed to have a wonderful long talk, not only about Hamlet and Shakespeare, but about any number of other mutually interesting subjects. And she wouldn't hesitate and grope for words at all. She would talk freely and easily, like Pam, only maybe a little more seriously. And Mike would say at last, "Penny, when we met this afternoon, I had no idea we'd be so congenial. I'm glad we had this chance to get really acquainted. We must see a lot of each other from now on."

Penny sighed a deep, ecstatic sigh and pushed open the library door. Mrs. Kenyon, the older of the two librarians, was at the desk. She gave Penny an impersonal smile, her eyes a little tired behind rimless spectacles. Penny smiled back at her, purposely keeping her glance from straying to the big table in the corner, where she had dreamed Mike might be. She didn't look toward it all the time she was locating a volume of Shakespeare on the shelves, one with a good, informative foreword about the author. With the book under her arm, Penny turned at last toward the reading corner. Mike wasn't there. She had known he wouldn't be and yet there was a small absurd ache of disappointment within her just the same.

"It serves you right," she told herself severely, "dreaming up fantastic things like that, stuff there isn't the remotest chance may happen."

She took her book over to the reading corner and sat down. No one else was at the table except a rather plump blond girl in a gabardine jacket. She looked sort of familiar, but Penny couldn't think where she had seen her. Then she noticed a volume of Shakespeare in front of the girl and realized it might have been in English class.

The girl's look half-recognized Penny, too. Finally she said, "Aren't you in Jensen's third period English?"

Penny nodded. "I thought I'd seen you before. I'm Penny Howard."

"New this year, aren't you?" the plump girl asked. She had a friendly smile. "I'm Jean Dickey. Can you imagine Jensen giving us such a stinking assignment the very first day of school?"

"Well—it doesn't have to be in till next week," Penny reminded her.

"I know," Jean said, "but Shakespeare—golly Moses! I mean, he's been dead so long and all."

Penny said, "That's one trouble with all the Elizabethan dramatists, I'm afraid."

Both girls laughed then, quite subdued laughter which didn't even reach Mrs. Kenyon's ears.

"Tell me," Jean Dickey said, leaning confidentially nearer, so that her shoulder brushed Penny's, "haven't you got a sister who looks just like you?"

Penny nodded. "We're twins. Her name's Pamela—Pam for short."

"Gee," the other girl said, "I should think that would be fun, having a twin."

"It is," Penny admitted. Inaudibly she added, "Usually." But tonight wasn't one of the times.

"Didn't I see you riding in Randy Kirkpatrick's car this afternoon?" Jean pressed, like a busy little vacuum cleaner picking up every bit of information she could. "Both of you? With him and Mike Bradley?"

"Yes," Penny said, "they gave us a lift home."

There was no mistaking the envious admiration in Jean's glance. "Lucky!" she said. "I wish those big wheels even knew I was alive. How'd you get acquainted with them so fast?"

"They're in my sister's math class," Penny explained.

Jean shook her head ruefully. "Randy's in my science lab period, but that doesn't mean he pays any attention to me. The Kirkpatricks are one of the richest families in town. They live in that great big English style house on Park Lane. You know the one? And Randy's an only child. He gets just about everything he wants."

"I suspected that," Penny admitted, "from the convertible. It's lush."

Jean sighed. "I've never been in it." She added then, informatively, "Laurie McGregor's got him pretty well sewed up—or anyway, she did last year."

Penny wondered who Laurie McGregor was. Or where she was, or had been that afternoon, at any rate. But she didn't have to ask. Jean went on to enlighten her. "Laurie's not back to school yet. She goes to Canada late every summer on account of her hay fever and she won't be home till the end of this week."

This would be news for Pam. Personally Penny didn't care too much one way or the other. It was Mike Bradley she was mainly interested in. But she couldn't bring herself to ask Jean whether Mike, too, had a regular girl. She tried to find comfort in the memory of Pam saying, "There's a kind of gleam in their eyes that usually indicates a free man." But if Pam were wrong about Randy, she could be wrong about Mike, too.

Penny asked herself coldly, "What possible difference does it make? Obviously Mike isn't interested in me, whether he's got another girl or not."

She gave Jean a little smile and patted the volume of Shakespeare on the table before her. "Don't you suppose we'd better get down to business, if we want to get that English assignment off our minds?"

"Yeah," Jean nodded glumly, "I guess so. . . ."

When Penny got home, Gran had gone to bed, but Mother was lying on the couch, glancing through a new magazine. There was no sign of Pam, nor of Randy.

"They went for a little ride," Mother answered Penny's inquiring look. "Just out to get a hamburger."

"Oh," Penny said. She asked then, "Didn't you like him?"

Mother nodded, her blue eyes thoughtful on Penny's face. "He seemed very nice."

As Penny turned toward her bedroom, Mother asked, "Penny, will you tell me something? Did you make a

point of going to the library tonight because Randy Kirkpatrick was coming over?"

"Why—well, yes," Penny had to admit it.

Mother said, still questioningly, "But I don't see just
why, dear. It wasn't as if Pam had a date with him, or
anything of that sort. He was simply bringing her book
back."

Penny nodded. "But—with me gone it developed into a
—a sort of date anyway. He took her out for a hamburger
and a ride and all."

"And if you'd stayed home?" Mother pressed.

"It would have been—awkward," Penny said. "There
I'd be, sticking up like a sore thumb. He'd have had to
ask us both, or neither one of us. And there was no point
in my messing things up for Pam, just by being here, when
I had this English assignment to do anyway. It wasn't,"
she added definitely, "as if I wanted to stick along with
them, as if it made the slightest bit of difference to me one
way or the other." She smiled at Mother then and blew
her a little kiss from the tips of her fingers. "'Night, now."

"Good night, dear," Mother said. But her tone still
sounded a little doubtful.

Chapter Five

A TALK WITH MOTHER

$\mathcal{I}$N ONLY a short while Penny had learned her way around Glen High quite thoroughly. No longer did her surroundings seem strange. She learned which teacher went with which subject. Now, less than two weeks since the first day of school, as she waited for Pam outside the entrance, she saw many familiar faces from one class or another. She smiled and spoke and was spoken to. That absurd sense of being invisible didn't trouble her at all.

Already both Pam and Penny were fairly well known among their classmates. Just as Pam had predicted, the very fact of their being twins gave them a certain distinction. Heads frequently turned as they passed along the halls together and speculative glances seemed to wonder which was which. Pam didn't mind this at all, but Penny felt a little embarrassed. Sometimes she thought it wasn't quite fair to deliberately confuse people by dressing just alike, by parting their dark hair on the same side and brushing it back from their faces in an identical manner.

But when she said as much, Pam demanded, "Why in the world not? I get a bang out of confusing people—it's half the fun of being twins." She chuckled then. "Mike says I'm an exhibitionist, but you don't see him holding it against me."

Penny had to admit that this was true. Still she argued, "But they know us apart right away when we start talking."

Pam nodded thoughtfully. "They wouldn't have to, though," she pointed out, "if you'd just pay a little attention to what I tell you. The thing is, Penny, you take things too seriously. Conversation doesn't have to make much sense. You just say anything that comes into your mind, without thinking too much about it. You see what I mean?"

Penny shook her head regretfully. "Nothing comes into my mind—nothing worth saying out loud, that is."

"But that's just the point," Pam assured her. "It doesn't have to be worth saying. Prittle-prattle, that's what I give 'em. And they love it!"

"I can't do it, though," Penny argued. "Honestly, I can't, Pam. I try—but I get all stuttery."

Pam patted her shoulder affectionately. "You have to relax," she told Penny, "not make such a big thing of it. If you could just get over being self-conscious. . . ."

That was the trouble, Penny knew. But how did one go about getting over it? Pam didn't have any very constructive ideas about that, Pam, who had never had an uncertain self-conscious moment in her life, who had enough poise and assurance for both of them, if it could only have been divided equally.

Standing in the crisp fall sunshine, waiting for her sister, Penny reflected that life would have been much more agreeable if Pam's self-confidence had been divided between the two of them. More agreeable for her, at any rate, Penny thought with a little smile. Of course, Pam wouldn't have liked it so well.

"Hi, Penny." Jean Dickey's friendly voice broke into her abstraction. "Come on and I'll walk to your corner with you."

Penny said, "I'm sorry, but I'm waiting for Pam. She ought to be along any minute. Won't you wait, too?"

Jean shook her blond head. "I don't think I'd better. I'm in kind of a rush. I see Maggie up ahead, I'll just catch up with her. See you." She was off down the steps in a fast lope.

Penny stared after her, saw her catch Maggie Wright just beyond the foot of the broad stone steps. The two girls strolled off together. Penny felt an absurd small thrust of disappointment, watching them go. If only Pam weren't always so pokey about getting to their appointed meeting place! It wasn't, Penny assured herself, that she wouldn't rather walk home with Pam than with Jean and Maggie. Pam was always fun to be with, aside from the fact of their being sisters. Penny had enjoyed being with Pam, ever since she could remember. "Two's company," Mother used to say about them with a little fond laugh when they were scarcely more than babies. "You two certainly bear out the truth of that old saying. Why, I think you could be perfectly happy and contented even if you never saw any one else."

It had always been that way. Penny supposed it always would be. Not that she didn't like to have girl friends. But there was a closeness, an understanding, between her and Pam that no other relationship could duplicate. Now if she and Pam and Jean and Maggie could all have walked home together, chattering and laughing and sharing secrets —that would have been lots of fun, Penny thought. But

Pam had confided to her privately that she didn't care too much for Jean and Maggie.

"There are other girls at school who are so much smoother," Pam had pointed out.

And Penny couldn't argue the point, she knew it was true. Still she felt easier with Jean and Maggie than she did with some of the girls Pam preferred. Susan Farnsworth and Gail Moore and Laurie McGregor. Now that was a queer thing, Penny reflected, shifting her books from one arm to the other. Pam's liking Laurie McGregor wasn't so strange, but Laurie McGregor's liking Pam—well, Penny considered that a little surprising. Of course, as Pam had pointed out to her, it wasn't as if Laurie and Randy had still been going steady when she, Pam, came into the picture.

"All that was over 'way back last June," Pam had informed Penny airily. "Randy told me so himself. So why should Laurie have a grudge against me just because Randy likes me a little?"

Pam made it all sound so logical.

"I guess I just don't have the proper perspective on these matters," Penny thought, casting a hopeful glance toward the opening door once again.

This time it was Pam, full of charming apologies for being late, apologies that started spilling over before Pam was scarcely through the opening. It was then Penny noticed the masculine hand on the door. Mike Bradley's big hand.

"Hi, Penny," Mike greeted her with his nice smile.

"Oh—hi," Penny said.

"Let's all go watch football practice for half an hour," Pam said, tucking her hand under Penny's elbow.

But Penny said stubbornly. "I don't want to watch football practice. You said you were going right home tonight, that you had a million things to do." She didn't mean to sound grumpy about it, but she had a lot of things to do herself. And Pam had said definitely—

"Oh, come on," Pam coaxed. "Mike twisted my arm, that's the only reason."

"I twisted *your* arm," Mike said with quite a different inflection. "All you want to watch for is so you can feast your eyes on that gorgeous hunk of man, Spark Mathews."

"Oh, Mike—you silly!" Pam said, laughing up at Mike across her shoulder. "You know Spark doesn't even know I'm alive."

"You know he is," Mike said. "That's what bothers me. Besides, Pamela, my pet, any guy with two eyes knows you're alive—and you don't see Spark wearing glasses. What," Mike demanded in mock despair, "has he got that I haven't besides muscles?"

"There now," Pam soothed, patting his hand. "I couldn't like you better if you were captain of the team. It's your intellect that wows me. Come on, Penny," she coaxed again. "Just half an hour."

But Penny shook her head. "Really, Pam," she insisted, "I've got to go. You do as you please."

She went down the long flight of stairs quickly, paying no attention to Pam's voice calling her name.

Hurrying down the street toward home, she thought, "I might as well have gone with Maggie and Jean."

But even walking home alone was better than spending half an hour watching Pam work on Mike Bradley. Of course, it wasn't only Mike Pam worked on. Randy Kirkpatrick, any number of other boys, knew equally well the heady spell of Pam's allurement. Pam could no more help bewitching whatever male she happened to be with than she could stop breathing. Delivery boys, store clerks, theater ushers, even male teachers, thawed visibly when Pam smiled at them. She could get away with murder, Penny knew, even where a lot of the female sex was concerned. "Certainly I can't hold out against her," Penny thought wryly. "And she has lots of girl friends."

Penny sighed a small sigh as she walked along, scuffling her feet through the dry leaves. It wasn't that she envied Pam her popularity. If only she could follow in her footsteps sufficiently to achieve a little of it for herself. . . .

When Penny let herself into the hallway at home, she listened for a minute to hear whether Mother was busy. Sometimes there would be so many customers in the shop Gran would be helping and the girls would pitch in and do whatever they could after school. But Mother was alone at the moment, riffling through a big book of wallpaper samples, a swatch of drapery material in one hand.

"Hi, honey," Mother hailed her, waving the swatch. "Never saw such a tough color to co-ordinate and Mrs. Bayliss has her heart set on it."

Penny went into the tastefully appointed salesroom and stood beside Mother, looking down at the big book. "Can't you persuade her to choose something more adaptable?"

Mother shook her head, laughing a little. "She feels this color expresses her personality or something. So, naturally, I have to go along with the idea."

Mother always made her problems sound like some sort of lark. But Penny knew there were a lot of headaches and plain hard work connected with the interior decorating business. She asked now, her tone sympathetic, "Is it a big job?"

"She's just doing over one room," Mother said. "But you can't slight the little jobs, Penny. They often pave the way for big ones."

Penny nodded. "I suppose so," she said. Then, "Pam stayed to watch football practice."

"Oh?" Mother's voice went up inquiringly. "Didn't you want to watch, too?"

"Not 'specially," Penny said. "She was with Mike. I'd have felt as if I were—sort of sticking along."

"Oh," Mother said, smoothing the soft nap of the drapery material through her fingers.

"Besides," Penny went on quickly, "we've got a Trigonometry test to cram for tomorrow. And I'd like to get that out of the way fairly early, so we can go to a club meeting tonight at school. If," she added, "I can get Pam to go to the club meeting."

"What sort of club?" Mother asked, her gaze thoughtful.

Penny explained, "There were notices on the bulletin board about a lot of club meetings. You see, they're all getting their memberships set for this year. The one tonight is called the Headlines Club. It's for people who are interested in working on the school paper."

"And you'd like that?" Mother asked.

Penny nodded, her eyes brightening. "I don't know how good I'd be, but it sounds like fun. I'm getting a big bang out of my journalism class."

"But you think Pam may not be interested?" Mother's tone was serious.

"Well—I don't know," Penny admitted ruefully. "She

doesn't like to read nearly as much as I do. And themes are hard for her, but I really like doing them. Pam thought it would be fun if we joined the Pep Club—that's the bunch they choose the cheer leaders from. But we were cheer leaders last year at our old school and I didn't care much for it. So I thought maybe I could persuade Pam to try the Headlines Club anyway and see how she liked it."

Mother continued to regard Penny thoughtfully. After awhile she asked, "Penny, tell me, are you and Pam happy out here in Glenhurst?"

"Oh, yes," Penny said, surprised that Mother should even think of asking such a question. "It's so much nicer, living the way we do now, with you home most of the time."

Mother reached out to give her hand a little affectionate squeeze. "I'm glad, dear. Certainly I'm a lot happier. But I was afraid you and Pam might feel I'd uprooted you from your old school, from all your friends."

Penny assured her, "Both of us like Glen High. And we're making new friends. Of course, we always have each other to fall back on. That's one of the nice things about being a twin. You're never all alone."

"No," Mother agreed, "you're not. But, Penny—" she was frowning a little, "you shouldn't depend too much on Pam. I don't think that would be a good thing for either of you."

"I don't," Penny said. "That is—I try not to."

Mother said gently, "I can see it isn't always easy for you. Pam is so—so—" she groped for the right word.

"So much more popular," Penny supplied, her voice low.

Mother's blue eyes widened. "That wasn't what I meant at all," she said firmly. "Forceful was the word I had in mind. Pam is forceful, but you mustn't let her influence you too strongly. You don't want to simply copy Pam, just because you happen to look alike."

"I wish I could be like her, inside as well as out," Penny admitted. She found herself going on, pouring out to Mother things she'd never had a chance to discuss with her before, or at least not since the need for discussion had arisen. In the city, when Mother had been away at her job all day, Penny had hated to bother her with problems at night when she was tired. Nor were they the sort of problems she'd cared to inflict on Gran, who had enough on her hands just taking care of the family's physical needs. Now Penny told Mother wistfully, "I think it would be the most wonderful thing in the world to be gay and vivacious like Pam, to be able to talk with boys without wondering what to say next, never bumbling around and getting all stiff and self-conscious. You know how she is, so easy and assured. And you've seen how everyone likes her, how the boys gather around—"

"Penny, wait—" Mother's voice was troubled, breaking in. "I can't deny Pam's popular. But that's because she's herself, a definite personality. You shouldn't try to copy her. You must be yourself, establish your own identity, not just go trailing along in Pam's wake."

Penny stood there, staring at Mother blankly. Not copy Pam, not try in every way she could to be like her? Such a thought had never occurred to Penny before.

Mother was going on, still in that troubled, but firm, tone. "You're you, Penny. If you're more quiet than Pam, that's nothing to fret over. Maybe you're quiet sometimes because you aren't vitally interested in the things Pam talks about. Maybe if the subject under discussion were important to you, it would be quite different. You must give yourself a chance to find your own interests, not just follow after Pam because you happen to be sisters. Take this club meeting tonight—ask Pam to go with you, but if she's not interested, go yourself. You're a person, too, darling. Never forget that."

Just then the outer door opened and Penny turned to see a middle-aged couple come in. Customers obviously. Mother gave her arm a little, reassuring pat as she moved away to wait on them. And Penny, a queer, tight feeling of breathlessness in her, left the salesroom to make her way quickly upstairs.

Chapter Six

THE CLUB MEETING

$\mathscr{I}$T WAS almost dinner time when Pam got home. Gran was in the kitchen. She had the little radio on and was singing a lively duet with Bing Crosby, so that the air was filled with music as well as delicious odors of cookery. Mother hadn't come upstairs yet. Although Howard House closed officially at five, there was often book work, or some other detail that kept Celia busy until much later.

Penny was setting the table in the dining alcove, arranging silverwear and bright-flowered china neatly on the yellow linen cloth. Pam came up behind her and asked winningly, "Mad at me?"

Penny shook her head. "Why should I be?"

"Oh," Pam said, "you went off in such a huff when I decided to watch football practice, I thought you might be."

"That was on account of the trig test tomorrow," Penny explained. "I had to study for it. You didn't forget all about it, did you?"

Pam's gray eyes widened in horror. "Golly Moses, I did! And I told Spark Mathews he could stop by later. A bunch of us walked home together after practice and Spark was quite friendly. We're going over to the Teen Hang-

56

out for a while—only, of course, Spark can't stay out very late, on account of being in training."

"Neither can you," Penny reminded drily. Only recently Mother had been driven to issue an ultimatum setting ten o'clock as the absolute limit on school nights.

"I know," Pam agreed. Suddenly her tone grew coaxing. "You can sort of brief me on the trig, can't you? So long as you've studied it? Just enough so I can get by."

"Well, I'll try," Penny said. "But we won't have too much time after dinner. I'm going to the Headlines Club at seven-thirty." She hurried on then at Pam's look of surprise, "I was going to ask you to go, too, but if you've already made a date with Spark Mathews—"

"But, Penny," Pam said in her most beguiling manner, "you don't want to waste time with that newspaper crowd. They're sort of droopy. The Pep Club will be a lot more fun. Laurie and Susan say they have perfectly hilarious times at their meetings."

Penny shook her head stubbornly. "I don't like cheer leading. You know I told you that last year, Pam."

"You don't have to be a cheer leader," Pam smiled at her. "It's just that the crowd's more fun."

"Maybe for you," Penny argued, "but I'd get more of a bang out of working on the paper."

Pam's eyes narrowed just a little. "Is it because Mike's editor?"

Penny stared at her blankly. "I didn't know he was."

"Well, he is," Pam informed her. "He wanted me to go to Headlines tonight, but I couldn't see it. I mean, there's no point in pretending to be interested in things you don't give a darn about, just because some boy—"

"I'm not doing that!" Penny denied hotly. "I didn't even know Mike had anything to do with it."

"Oh, I didn't mean you," Pam assured her. "I was just talking. You go right ahead to your club meeting—I imagine one's all it'll take to prove how boring it is." She strolled off toward their bedroom.

Penny called after her, "Why don't you study some now? It'll probably be half an hour before we eat."

"Oh, I can't now," Pam called back. "I have to do my nails. They're a mess. Penny," she inquired then, "did you know Spark's six feet three tall? And such shoulders—I wouldn't believe them if I hadn't seen them close-up."

Mike was six feet tall, Penny thought dreamily. And he had very nice shoulders, too. A little thrill of anticipation stirred in her at the thought of seeing him at Headlines. She was glad now that she had decided to take Mother's advice and go. It hadn't been an easy decision for Penny to reach. She had sat on her bed, her school books spread out around her, for quite a long while before she actually began to study trigonometry. The habit of following after Pam, of doing the things Pam was interested in, was too strong to be easily broken. But tonight, Penny had made up her mind, would be a starting point at least. She was going to hold out against Pam's coaxing, her winning charm. She'd probably backslide pretty often, but at least she was going to make an effort to establish herself as a person in her own right, with interests and activities apart from Pam. Being a carbon copy hadn't worked out so well. Maybe Mother's solution of the problem would prove more effective. The only way to find out was to give it a try.

"Penny," Pam's wheedling voice broke into her reflections, "come help me with trig while I do my nails. And

I'll try to get home in time to do some more studying later."

"Well—okay," Penny agreed. Having taken a firm stand about the club meeting, she guessed she could afford to be magnanimous about unimportant details. . . .

Just as Penny walked into the Journalism Room, where the Headlines meeting was to be held, she felt a big hand grab her arm and heard Mike Bradley's agreeably surprised voice, saying, "Pam, you did decide to come after all!"

Penny shook her head, looking up at him, an uncertain smile on her lips. "Sorry, Mike. I'm Penny."

"Oh," Mike's disappointment was obvious and unflattering. His grip on her arm relaxed, as he added ruefully, "I thought it was funny she passed up Muscle-man Mathews. But for a minute there you had me fooled." He wagged his head toward a couple of empty seats. "Might as well sit down. The meeting's due to get under way."

There were many familiar faces in the big, talk-filled room. Penny saw most of the people from her journalism class. Mrs. Gebhard, the journalism teacher, who was also the club's faculty advisor, was there, too.

Sitting in the chair next to Mike's even if he wasn't paying much attention to her, Penny was glad she had come.

Mike leaned his elbows on his knees and stared glumly straight ahead of him. Penny surmised he was brooding over Pam's date with Spark Mathews. She wished she could think of something interesting to say, something that would make him notice her. But before she was able to, Mrs. Gebhard stood up and called the meeting to order.

Immediately Penny found her attention absorbed. This wasn't dull and boring at all, as Pam had so confidently predicted. There was quite a bit of discussion of the inner workings of the school weekly, which was called the *Glen Crier*. The circulation manager announced an impending drive for subscriptions. Mike Bradley, as editor, announced the need for a few more reporters, besides those chosen the previous spring. He suggested that anyone willing to do some leg work, running down news items around the school, sign his or her name on a list that had been provided for the purpose.

"I could do that," Penny thought. "It would be fun."

So afterward, while Mike was absorbed in conversation with a couple of other boys, Penny went over to sign her name on the list on Mrs. Gebhard's desk.

The journalism teacher smiled at her. "You should make a good reporter, Penny," Mrs. Gebhard remarked. "You have quite a nice flair for writing."

"Why—why, thank you," Penny stammered, a warm glow enveloping her at the unexpected compliment.

Maggie Wright came up behind her then. Maggie was a small dark-haired girl, with straight bangs and a forthright manner.

She said, "Hi, Penny. Glad you're signing up."

"I may be pretty much of a dub," Penny said. "I've never done any reporting before."

"I'm an old hand," Maggie chuckled. "There's nothing to it. Most people are anxious to tell you All if there's a chance they'll get to see their names in print. And, of course, there are always club meetings and junk like that to fill in with."

"Yes, I suppose so," Penny agreed. "It doesn't sound too complicated."

"You shoving off now?" Maggie asked. Then, at Penny's nod, "We can walk together, maybe stop at the Hangout for a Coke."

Penny hesitated only a second before saying, "Sure, that would be fine." In that intervening instant her glance had slipped unobtrusively to Mike Bradley, who was surrounded now by a group of half a dozen talking, laughing girls and boys. Penny jibed at herself as she linked arms with Maggie, "Did you imagine he'd be watching for a chance to walk home with you? How silly can you get, for creep's sake?" Aloud she said to Maggie, no trace of her disappointment sounding in her voice, "A Coke would hit the spot."

The Hangout was crowded till its very walls seemed threatened, and noisy as usual. Juke box music and conversation and shouts of laughter were all stirred up together into a deafening brew. The booths around the sides were filled to over-flowing, so Penny and Maggie stood with their drinks in the genial press of people around the soda fountain. It was nearing closing time, ten o'clock on week nights, and the effervescent gayety seemed to be rising in a sort of crescendo. There was even a not unpleasant rhythm about it, Penny thought, listening and smiling a little, as she sipped her drink.

"Hi, Penny!" She heard Pam's voice from halfway down the room and waved back at her. Pam was in one of the most crowded booths, Spark Mathews' massive shoulders almost shutting her off from Penny's view.

"You want to go back there?" Maggie asked, her dark eyes level.

But Penny shook her head. "She's with Spark and a bunch of other couples. I'd rather go on home when we finish our drinks."

So that was what they did, strolling along the well-lighted street together to within half a block of Penny's house, where Maggie had to turn off. They stood there under a street light, talking for a few minutes more about the club meeting, then said good night and went their respective ways.

When Penny let herself into the house, she heard voices from upstairs. In the living room Gran and Lucius Hancock were playing cribbage. There was nothing at all unusual about this. Mr. Hancock dropped in often to see the Howards and, whatever his reason for coming, he and Gran usually got out the cards and the little pegged wooden board before the evening was over.

"Hello, dear." Gran gave Penny a rather preoccupied smile.

"Hello, Pam, or Penny, as the case may be." This was Mr. Hancock's customary greeting to either of the twins.

Answering, Penny was struck anew by the contrast between Mr. Hancock's venerable white head and the youthfully dazzling sport shirts he affected. Almost before the words were out of her mouth, Gran and Mr. Hancock were concentrating once more on their game.

"That's a very cut-throat competition," Mother chuckled. She was curled up on the couch, listening to the tail-end of a news broadcast. She reached out one hand to switch it off, then indicated the big bowl of popcorn on the coffee table. "Have some, honey?"

Penny helped herself, then perched on the arm of the couch beside Mother. "The club meeting was lots of fun," she said. And proceeded to tell Mother all about it with contagious enthusiasm.

"Well, fine," Mother smiled when she finished. "I'm

glad you're going to be a reporter, so long as you like writing."

"I don't know how much actual writing I'll get to do," Penny admitted. "Maybe it'll be just gathering news items. But anyway, I think I'll enjoy it."

They talked for a little while longer, then Penny said good night and wandered off to her bedroom. She didn't turn on the light just at first, but stood for a dreaming moment at the window, looking out into the night. It seemed, she thought, almost like Fate that she and Mike Bradley should both be interested in writing. Because, naturally, Mike couldn't have been made editor of the *Crier*, if he hadn't done a good deal of earlier work along that line. Editor was a big job, an important one. Penny felt a little absurd glow of pride to think of Mike's having been chosen to fill the post. Maybe, working on the paper even in a small capacity, she'd be able to learn from Mike. At least, they should be thrown together to some extent. Take tonight, for instance. Just because she'd gone to Headlines, she'd got to sit next to him, to talk with him casually. She tried to push out of her mind the memory of the way his face had fallen at the realization that she wasn't Pam.

"I won't think about that!" Her lips formed the words fiercely, but silently.

She pulled the draw-drapes at the window then and turned away from it. Lighting the dresser lamps in their stiff plaid gingham shades, she proceeded to get ready for bed. There didn't seem to be much point in turning off the lights. Pam should be home any minute. It was after ten now.

But long after Penny had got into bed and fallen asleep, Pam still hadn't come.

Chapter Seven

THE DECEPTION

THE ALARM clock shrilled and Penny reached a languid hand to silence it, then snuggled back under the covers for that delicious last five minutes. Finally she leaned across and shook the bump that was Pam's shoulder in the bed beside hers. "Hey, wake up!"

Muffled grunts indicated that the mere idea of awaking filled Pam with profound distaste. But she emerged from her cocoon sufficiently to regard Penny with one eye. That was at least a step in the right direction. Pam was never an easy riser.

Penny swung her feet over the side of her bed and found her beat-up lamb's-wool slippers. Stretching and yawning, she went to the windows and pulled back the drapes. Sunlight brightened the charming room, with its maple furniture and perky gingham accents.

Grinning, Penny asked, "How late were you last night?"

"Don't ask!" Pam emerged a bit farther from the covers to moan. "It was awful! After I saw you at the Hangout, we all decided to go for a little ride. And when we were 'way out in the country, Spark's jalopy had a flat. And he doesn't even own a spare!"

"How did you get home?" Penny asked, appalled.

"Walked miles to a filling station," Pam told her. "My

feet still ache. One of the boys called his father and he drove out and picked us up. It was after one when I got home and Mother was simply fit to be tied."

"What a shame," Penny said.

Her eye lit on the clock then and she headed for the bathroom. They had a standing agreement that whoever was up first in the morning had inalienable rights to the first shower. This morning, Penny had a hunch, Pam wouldn't even mind.

When Penny came out of the bathroom, Pam lifted herself on one elbow to stare owlishly from beneath her tumbled hair. "What we wearing today?" she asked. "It's your turn to choose."

"Let's be different for a change," Penny suggested.

But Pam groaned, "Don't you start giving me trouble. I've already got the screaming meemies thinking of that trig test!"

"That's right!" Penny exclaimed in belated realization. "You were going to study when you got home last night."

"Exactly." Pam struggled out of bed and stood up, stretching. "I was going to get in early and cram for it."

Penny didn't remind her that she could have declined to go for the ride. There seemed no point in that now. And circumstances certainly had conspired to give Pam trouble. Penny felt genuinely sorry for her.

Suddenly a speculative gleam flared in Pam's eye. She smiled warmly at Penny and her tone took on a beguiling note. "Darling, I've got the most perfectly terrific idea."

"What about?" Penny asked distrustfully. She'd been charmed by Pam too often not to recognize the initial stages of one of her big operations.

"The trig test," Pam said slowly. "Wouldn't it be silly

to let me flunk it when you're well enough prepared for us both?"

Penny frowned. "What are you getting at?"

"It would be so simple," Pam said winningly, "for you just to take the test twice."

"Oh, no!" Penny exclaimed positively.

"But why not, Pen? You have trig second period and I don't have it till fifth. We could get away with it perfectly well. You have study hall fifth period, don't you?"

"Yes, but—"

"Well, then, you see?" Pam spread her hands expansively. "You needn't even risk my letting you down in one of your own subjects. I can easily fill in for you in study hall without anyone catching on."

"But it wouldn't be honest," Penny objected.

"Why is it so different," Pam coaxed, "if you help me study for tests, as you always do, or whether you be a perfect angel and take just this one for me?"

"There's a lot of difference," Penny said firmly. "This would be cheating, pure and simple."

"Ah, Pen. I've done lots of favors for you."

Penny could feel her determination not to weaken faltering a little under the impact of Pam's pleading. When Pam really went to work on you resistance wasn't easy.

"I'll be in a jam if I flunk the test," Pam went on sorrowfully. "You know how shakey I am in math. I might not get a passing grade for the whole semester. And it's not as if last night were my fault. I really meant to get home early and study."

"I can't do it, Pam," Penny insisted. "I'd help you in any way I could. But Mr. Williams would be sure to realize I wasn't you and we'd both be in all kinds of trouble."

"No, he wouldn't," Pam coaxed. "No one would."

"Mike and Randy can tell us apart," Penny said. "They're in your class."

"If you got in at the last minute," Pam told her, "they couldn't speak to you till afterward. Besides, even if they suspected we'd done a switch, they wouldn't give us away. Please, Penny?"

But Penny shook her head firmly in the negative.

Still, Pam didn't give up. All the time she was in the shower, she kept calling out new arguments over the hiss and spatter of the water. And when she came out of the bathroom, she took in what Penny was wearing with an appraising eye, then headed for the closet to select identical clothes. "Just in case you decide to save my life after all," she said winningly.

Following her out to breakfast, Penny tried to steel herself anew. The insidious thing about Pam's charm was the way it could make you doubt your own convictions, make you wonder if maybe you were being stuffy and unreasonable after all.

On the way to school Pam worked ceaselessly on Penny. She had an answer for every one of Penny's arguments. Her most telling point was that she might fail in trig if she flunked this test; she might not even graduate.

It was like water wearing away stone by dripping constantly upon it. The habit of helping Pam, of doing as she wanted, was so deeply ingrained in Penny, that gradually she felt the foundations of her resistance melting away. At last she gave into the extent of saying, "Well, I'll see, Pam. I'll think about it."

She found herself thinking of little else that day, moving from class to class as in a bad dream. Several teachers remarked about her unaccustomed abstraction. And every time she encountered her sister, Pam exerted a bit more irresistible pressure. Finally, knowing it was wrong, but unable to withstand Pam's coaxing any longer, Penny agreed to do as her sister wished.

As she slipped into Pam's seat in trig class that afternoon, seconds ahead of the bell, Penny's sense of guilt was so overwhelming, she almost wished Mr. Williams would see that a deception was being practiced upon him. How had she ever let herself be talked into this, she wondered wildly? A mad instinct toward flight flared up in her, but it was too late now. She was trapped here in Pam's seat, wrapped in Pam's identity. Anything she did now to destroy the illusion that she was Pam would get both of them into serious trouble. As she sat cowering there, her heart shaking her with its nervous beating, she caught Laurie McGregor's eye from across the aisle. Laurie smiled at her in friendly unsuspicious fashion, even leaned over to speak.

But Penny was saved by Mr. Williams, saying in his most scholarly manner, "All right, class. Let's get right down to business. The test questions are on these papers I'm going to pass out."

Penny's pen moved almost automatically, answering questions quite similar to those she had answered in her own class earlier. Her handwriting was so like Pam's, Penny knew, that it would have taken a most observing and suspicious eye to detect the difference. And why should the teacher suspect that anything was being put over on him? Why should anyone doubt that she was Pam?

It wasn't fear of discovery that made Penny spend the

longest and most miserable hour of her whole life in the math room. Her conscience wouldn't let her forget for a minute the dishonest thing she was doing. Still, when the papers had been collected and the bell ending the period had rung, Penny felt an upsurging of relief. Guilt-ridden as she was, at least the shameful thing was over and done with now. All she need do was escape. And try to forget.

Laurie McGregor paused to talk with Randy Kirkpatrick and for that Penny was grateful. She didn't want to get involved in conversation with anyone. It wouldn't be safe. Penny hurried toward the door, but just short of it she felt a detaining hand on her arm and glanced up fearfully into Mike Bradley's frowning face.

"What's your rush, Pam?" Mike's tone held a note of sarcasm. "Aren't you speaking to anybody but football heroes now?"

Penny gulped, "Why, yes, of course, Mike. I—just didn't see you."

"Don't hand me that," Mike growled. "What's the pitch? You rushing off to meet Spark somewhere?"

Penny looked at him through her lashes in what she hoped was Pam's melting, beguiling way. "Why, Mike, you silly," she breathed reproachfully, just as Pam would have.

To her surprise, it worked. Mike's frown faded and an unwilling grin took its place. "Maybe you were just trying to get away from the unpleasant smell of a trig test. Did it give you a lot of trouble?"

"Oh, no," Penny began, then broke off abruptly. She couldn't imagine Pam admitting she hadn't had trouble with a test of any kind. "That is," she amended hastily, "it wasn't too bad."

Mike's brows lifted a little in surprise. And at that exact second, Penny heard Mr. Williams' voice behind her, saying, "Miss Howard, will you come here a minute?"

She actually swayed, she was brought up so suddenly by the teacher's words. Fear of discovery spurted through her veins like ice water. What had she done to arouse Mr. Williams' suspicion? Could she have made such an utterly stupid error as signing her name "Penny" instead of "Pam"?

Her heart hammering, she made her way through the crowd of departing students to the teacher's desk. Mr. Williams, whose tall lanky build and short haircut gave him a deceptively youthful look, stood with one bony hand resting on the stack of test papers. One fearful glance assured Penny that hers wasn't the one on top.

"What about that past-due assignment?" the teacher asked.

Penny said in a sort of gulp, "I—I'm sorry, but I don't have it today." Darn Pam anyway! Why hadn't she told her?

Mr. Williams asked gravely, "And what did you promise me yesterday, Miss Howard?"

What had Pam promised, Penny wondered wildly? That she'd bring in the assignment today? That seemed logical, still—Penny murmured, as indefinitely as possible, "I'm terribly sorry, but with the test and all—" her voice sort of ran down.

Mr. Williams said, "Speak up, Miss Howard. I can't hear your excuse. It's not like you to be at a loss for words."

Not like you? Penny felt as if she were choking.

Then Mike's voice said, just behind her, "Pam, you'd

better hurry. We'll be late for—" he broke off then, embarrassed. "Oh, I'm sorry, Mr. Williams. I didn't realize Pam was talking to you."

Never had an interruption been so timely! Penny was able to gather her wits sufficiently to apologize again, to promise to get the assignment in tomorrow without fail. With Mike to lend moral support, she even managed to smile up at the teacher, just as Pam would have done.

To her astonishment Mr. Williams smiled back and let her go with only a, "Well, don't forget again, Miss Howard."

Not until she was safe outside the math room door did Penny expel her breath in a long sigh of relief.

"Okay, kid," Mike said, his voice low, "you can drop the disguise now. I won't give you away."

Penny stared up at him, her eyes wide. "You know?"

Mike nodded, glancing around to be sure no one was within hearing distance. "I began to suspect when you said the test wasn't bad. Then when you got so scared over old Williams calling you back—well, I caught on for sure. Pam isn't scared of Williams. She's got him wrapped around her finger. It's just when he dishes out test grades she gets worried."

"Then," Penny said gratefully, "you only called me Pam in front of him to help me out?"

"That was the Marines landing," Mike grinned at her.

"You certainly saved my life," Penny admitted. "I was getting all bogged down over that past-due assignment."

"How did she get you to pinch-hit for her?" Mike's tone was suddenly grave. "It's not a very honest thing to do."

Flushing painfully, Penny found herself pouring out the whole story, telling Mike about the flat tire, about Pam's worries over failing math. She finished, looking up into his eyes for a candid moment, "And you know how persuasive Pam can be."

"You, too?" Mike's grin was wry. "I thought maybe constant exposure carried some kind of immunity. But if you can't hold out against her—"

"I will after this," Penny said firmly. There was a determined set to her chin as she and Mike walked down the corridor side by side. "I won't ever get involved in anything like this again."

"It's a pretty shady business," Mike agreed. "You could get into a bad jam, both of you."

"I know," Penny nodded miserably. "But it isn't only the idea of getting caught. I feel so awful inside, so ashamed and sorry. And I got so scared, talking to Mr. Williams, I felt as if I was going to faint."

"It showed, too," Mike said, with a little chuckle. "For a second there, I thought I was going to have to catch you."

But Penny couldn't laugh about it, couldn't say anything more for the hurting lump in her throat. When they reached the angle of the hall where their paths parted, Mike gave her shoulder a little comforting pat.

"Better forget the whole thing," he told her. "Your secret's safe with me. Be seeing you."

Penny felt abjectly grateful for his kindness. And watching Mike stride off toward his next class, she realized with a little shock of surprise that she had been talking to him without the slightest trace of self-consciousness. For a moment she wondered that this should be so. Then her troubling sense of guilt wiped out any slight satisfaction she might otherwise have felt.

Chapter Eight

A SORT OF FRIENDSHIP

*L*ATER that day, telling Pam all about it, Penny admitted, "I never felt so low and guilty over anything in my whole life! And if it hadn't been for Mike, stepping in at the crucial moment, we'd have been caught—not that I'd care much, the way I feel."

"There now," Pam soothed, "take it easy. I'm sorry I got you onto such thin ice. But I forgot all about the darned assignment." At Penny's accusing look, she added, "I guess it was wrong to ask you to take the test for me. But, gee, Pen, I was scared I'd flunk. Can't we just forget the whole thing now?"

"Maybe you can," Penny said unhappily.

The twins were out in the big side yard of Howard House, in jeans and flannel shirts, raking up the leaves that lay all about in brown and gold profusion. Penny rather liked the job, but Pam kept looking up hopefully in case some boy she knew might be passing by, one to whom she could delegate her share of it.

Loading leaves onto the little metal cart in which she would wheel them out to the rubbish burner for disposal, Penny said grimly, "There's one point I want to make absolutely clear. I'll never do a thing like that again, never as long as I live."

"I won't ask you to," Pam promised. Then, a demon of

mischief dancing in her eyes, she added, "But I hope you got me a good grade."

Penny glared at her over an armful of leaves. "Better than you deserve. And you'd better get that past-due assignment in tomorrow, as I promised."

"Don't worry about a thing," Pam said. "I can take care of routine matters like past-due assignments."

"So Mike told me," Penny's tone was dry.

"Oh, he did, did he?" Pam stopped raking and her gray eyes narrowed just a little. "Any other gems of inside information Mr. Mike Bradley had to pass on to you about me?"

"Well, he did say," Penny couldn't help telling her, "that he thought I ought to be immune to letting you talk me into things, after all the years I've been exposed to you."

"What a charming thought," Pam drawled. "Makes me sound like measles or something."

"It didn't the way Mike said it," Penny had to admit.

"How did he say it?" Pam pressed.

"As if he's had some trouble resisting you himself."

"Well, good," Pam nodded a trifle smugly, leaning on her rake. "I'll wear him down all right. It's just a matter of time."

Penny didn't like the little confident smile that played around Pam's mouth as she said that. . . .

During the weeks that followed, Pam worked on Mike harder than ever. She didn't concentrate on him exclusively. That wasn't Pam's way. She liked a lot of attention, from a lot of boys. And she had no trouble getting it. Randy Kirkpatrick, quietly attractive and with an apparently unlimited amount of spending money, took her out most often. But big, amiably blustering Spark Mathews was with her whenever he could manage it, despite the fact that his being the mainstay of the football team made the feminine competition for his favor keen indeed. And Mike, too, although at first he made some effort to hold out against her charms, soon slipped as completely under Pam's spell as the others.

Penny guessed that even a degree of resistance to Pam's wiles was just too much to expect of any male. But Mike was the only one whose bedazzlement she found hard to take. If Mike could just have held out, Pam would have been so welcome to the rest of her admirers. Penny wouldn't have minded at all. Not that she let Pam know of her secret disappointment. Or Mike. Pride helped her keep her own deep liking for him a secret from Pam, close as they were. It wasn't easy, but Penny managed. Maybe, she told herself, it was a part of growing up to be able to keep things shut up inside of you. Sometimes she wondered whether Mother and Gran didn't suspect how she felt about Mike. But, if they did, they said nothing.

Mike and Spark and Randy came often to the Howard's. Sometimes, if two of them turned up at once, Pam would suggest that Penny come out with them for a soda or a hamburger or whatever casual entertainment was afoot. And sometimes Penny went and sometimes she didn't. She couldn't see that her presence mattered much, one way or the other. She didn't care, really, so far as Spark and Randy were concerned. They were pleasant enough company, but they meant little to her personally. With Mike it was different. With Mike it hurt to realize herself a fifth wheel.

But gradually, there came about a subtle shift in Mike's

attitude toward Penny. She became an individual to him, not just Pam's sister. Their work on the school paper threw them together to a considerable extent and in circumstances quite apart from Pam's sphere of activity. Without Pam around to constantly overshadow her, Mike seemed to realize that Penny was a person, too. The fact that she proved to have a definite knack for reporting was another motivating factor in their changed relationship. Penny became for Mike, in his capacity as editor, a sort of ever-dependable Girl Friday. They worked together well as a team and Mike delegated to her all sorts of small, necessary jobs that were yet not sufficiently important to engage the time and attention of his assistant editor, owlishly solemn, caustic-tongued Bob Purcell. Penny didn't mind. Quite the contrary. Almost before either of them realized it, Penny and Mike had become friends in a casual sort of way.

Being friends with Mike was quite the most wonderful thing that had ever happened to Penny. Impersonal as their contacts were, she was grateful for Mike's liking. Never before had she felt so at ease with a boy, so untroubled by self-consciousness. She could talk with Mike, seriously or lightly, without getting all stuttery and embarrassed. Even the knowledge that Mike was aware of the most shameful act of her life no longer troubled Penny quite so deeply. That day she had substituted for Pam at the trig test still made a dark blot in Penny's mind. There had been times during the intervening weeks when she had felt almost unbearably driven to confess the whole shoddy business to Mother, or Gran. Only the knowledge that by so doing she would get Pam into trouble, too, deterred her. And

Mike seemed to have forgotten all about it, just as he had advised her to do. Penny supposed that was best.

She was grateful for the change in her relationship with Mike and determined to do everything she could to keep things on this new and infinitely more satisfactory basis. As for Mike, he treated her as he might have treated another boy—or a sister, perhaps. He bossed her around. He kidded her. He called her a dope for letting Pam impose on her. And, in an occasional brooding mood, he tried to worm out of her how he really stood with Pam.

Of course, Penny didn't feel in the least like a sister toward Mike. But that was her own affair. Friendship was better than nothing. So she kidded him back, thankful not to be ignored. And even the hurt of listening to Mike rave about Pam's charms was a small price to pay for the privilege of having him confide in her.

It was a shame, really, that Mike had fallen so hard for Pam. Thus Penny reflected one November day as she sat in the cluttered little alcove off the journalism room, which constituted the office of the *Glen Crier*. Penny was ostensibly writing up some notes on yesterday's Y-Teens meeting. But Mike was banging out an editorial on the typewriter just opposite her, so it was hard to keep her mind entirely on her work. Pam, Penny knew, was by no means sure she preferred Mike's company to that of Randy or Spark or the rest of the boys she dated. It had been different just at first, when Mike had seemed a shade standoffish and hard-to-get. Then Pam had really worked on him. Penny could have told Mike—only, of course, she wouldn't, that it was always that way with Pam. She'd try hard as anything to get a boy under her spell, then simply add him to her collection. Or she might decide she didn't want him after all.

"Is that what you're hoping will happen in Mike's case?" Penny asked herself sternly. "Do you imagine then you'll catch him on the rebound, just because you're friends after a fashion?"

She felt hot color creep across her face at the thought and bent her head determinedly to the job at hand, even if it was pretty much of a routine one.

"There now," Mike said, easing his paper out of the typewriter. "This takes care of next week. But good ideas for editorials are sure hard to come by. You don't happen to have any, do you?"

Penny glanced up at him thoughtfully. "I do have one you might be able to use later on."

"How much later?"

"Well, it's about the Prom."

"Prom stuff's for spring," Mike said. "But tell me."

"Some of the girls were griping about this at lunch. You know, Mike, it's really not very fair the way it is with the Prom," Penny said earnestly. "All the senior girls work on it like crazy, serve on committees and everything like that. Then it develops that a lot of them don't get to go to it. And you know why?"

"Because they don't get invited?" Mike suggested. "But they're free to invite dates of their own, you know."

"Yes, but who can they ask?" Penny demanded. "You know perfectly well lots of the senior men go and invite junior and soph girls. But if the senior girls asked younger fellows, they'd be accused of cradle snatching and kidded to death."

"Yeah," Mike admitted, "I suppose they would."

"Besides," Penny pointed out, "Prom tickets aren't cheap. You kind of hesitate to ask a man to assume a lot of expenses for a date when you ask him to take you. And if the girl pays, the boy feels silly. It's murder."

Mike scratched his head consideringly, his blue eyes thoughtful. "Yeah, I see your point. We might do a piece about that closer to Prom time—not that it'll probably do any good. Speaking of dances," he said then and Penny's heart skipped a beat, "tell me something. Is Pam already dated for the Sweater Hop?"

Penny's heart resumed its normal pace. She looked down at the tips of her loafers, just in case that flash of bright crazy hope might have left some reflection in her eyes for Mike to see. "Why—yes, she is. She's going with Spark."

"I just wanted to be sure," Mike nodded a trifle grimly. "I'll stay home and save my money."

Penny's eyes lifted to his face. "The Sweater Hop's not very expensive, is it? Informal, no corsage, just held in the gym."

"Any date with your sister," Mike informed her, "is likely to run into money. Of which, if you'll pardon a sordid mercenary note, I have very little at the moment. Not that I'm complaining," he hastened to add, "about your twin being an expensive woman, that is. She's worth it, believe me."

Penny frowned slightly, the familiar instinct to rush to Pam's defense rising within her. "You make her sound— not very nice," she accused.

"Simmer down now," Mike chuckled drily. "I didn't mean to razz Pam. Any woman's expensive to date very often. A movie here, hamburgers and sodas there, it all counts up. And my allowance is strictly from hunger. I'm looking around for an after-school job, but so far I haven't found one."

"But could you handle a job along with your school work and being editor of the *Crier* and all?" Penny asked.

"I'd be a busy little bee," Mike grinned. "But think of all the lovely green stuff I'd have to squander."

Bob Purcell came in then, said, "Hi," casually to Penny and dropped a sheaf of scrawled pages on Mike's desk. "There you are, slave driver. Once we get this stuff whipped into shape—"

As soon as she had finished writing up her club notes, Penny eased out of the door with a murmured, " 'Bye, now." Neither Mike nor Bob seemed to notice, so intent were they on their work. Penny stopped at her locker to get her coat and a couple of books. There were a few students still in the halls, but Penny didn't see anyone she knew well, anyone who might be walking home her way. She hadn't planned to meet Pam. Pam was a cheer leader now and busy this afternoon with a Pep Club meeting.

Walking along through the crisp fall sunshine, Penny felt a slight edge to the wind that whipped her hair backward from her face. Before long it would be winter, she thought. But Penny liked winter. The snow should be beautiful, out here away from the city's grime. Penny could see the white, unbroken expanses quite clearly in her mind. And there would be skating on the frozen lake back of the high school, and sleigh ride parties. Penny had never gone on a sleigh ride in her life. And her skating had been done on a city rink, with tall buildings in the background.

Oh, she was glad they'd moved to Glenhurst. She liked everything about it so much better than the city. The friendliness of neighbors, the more casual way of living, the opportunity that had been afforded her to see more of Mother, to get closer to her. She and Mother had had several good talks since that day when Mother had urged her to go to Headlines Club without Pam, if Pam didn't care to go. And because of these talks Penny felt she had come to see her problem a little more clearly and to make a beginning toward solving it.

Her job on the *Crier* was a step in the right direction, a big step. Pam thought she was silly to waste so much time on it. Pam didn't hesitate to tell her so. But Penny didn't consider it a waste. She enjoyed the work and through it a whole new circle of friends had been opened up to her. Besides Mike, there were lots of other people she liked on the *Crier* staff, people she enjoyed being with, people who accepted her as an individual, not just a sort of shadowy echo of Pam's more vivacious personality.

"To them," Penny reflected as she walked along, "I'm me, I'm an individual. I don't have to be forever trying to measure up to Pam. To Maggie and Bob and the others it doesn't matter that Pam has more dates than I. They accept me at face value, they seem to like me for myself. If I'd gone on trying to copy Pam, trailing after her into Pep Club, just because that was what she wanted to do, maybe I'd have got better acquainted with Laurie and Susan and the rest of the glamour crowd—but I'd have been just Pam's droopy twin to them. And Mike and I would never have been friends as we are—" Penny's thought broke at the pricking realization that they weren't good enough friends that it would occur to Mike to ask her to the Sweater Hop, since Pam was going with some-one else.

"Even so," Penny assured herself staunchly, "being myself is better."

Nothing was going to shake her hard-won certainty of that.

Chapter Nine

ALMOST A DATE

$\mathcal{G}$RAN finished a new sweater for Pam just in time for the Sweater Hop. It was a luscious lime green, which went perfectly with Pam's melon-colored pleated skirt. Gran had barely started Penny's matching sweater, but that didn't matter since Penny wasn't going to the Hop.

"You could have," Pam reminded her, "if you'd wanted to. Spark's boss, so far as the whole team's concerned. He could have got a date for you easily and we could have gone together."

"I know," Penny nodded. She was sitting cross-legged on her bed, in corduroy skirt and the slightly rumpled white blouse she had been wearing all that Saturday, watching Pam start to get ready for the dance. It was quite early yet, only around seven-thirty. But getting ready for a dance, even an informal school affair like the Sweater Hop, was a leisurely process with Pam. Right now she was fresh from her shower and just starting to take her hair out of curlers. She stood tall and intent before the dresser mirror, her yellow terry-cloth robe belted tightly around her slim middle, her bare feet thrust into lamb's-wool scuffs.

Now her eyes met Penny's in the mirror and she asked,

her tone sharpening a little, "Why do you say 'I know' in such a wistful sort of tone?"

"I didn't mean to sound wistful," Penny said. She really hadn't. Pam was imagining things. She went on, "I know you offered to have Spark get someone for me so we could double-date."

Pam turned her full attention to her curlers once more. "Well, then! I don't see why you wouldn't. Don't you like dances?"

"Of course," Penny admitted. Who didn't? She could imagine nothing more wonderful than to go to the Hop with Mike—if Mike had asked her. If anyone else within reason had asked her, she probably wouldn't have turned him down, either. But to have Pam tell Spark to get someone for her—well, she wasn't that eager to go.

Pam was frowning. "You'll hardly ever double-date any more like we used to. Why, Penny? What's got into you?"

Penny supposed Pam was entitled to an explanation. She told her, "It's not that I don't like double-dating. But the idea of you having your date drag someone along for me—well, can't you understand how unnecessary that makes me feel? If someone had asked me to the Hop, of his own accord, then I'd think it was fine for us to go with you and Spark. But the other way's no good."

Pam turned around slowly to look at her. "You never used to mind."

A wry little smile pulled at Penny's lips. "I minded. It was just—well, I was willing to let you fix up dates for me, rather than not getting to go places at all."

"And," Pam fingered the last curler out of her hair, her

gray eyes questioning, "you don't feel that way about it any more?"

"That's it," Penny admitted. "I guess maybe I've grown up. I seem to be reconciled to doing without dates, if I can't get them for myself."

"But that's silly!" Pam dumped the curlers into her dresser drawer impatiently. "Penny, it's that stuffy crowd you've got in with. They've warped your sense of values! You can't be content to simply work on the paper all the time!"

"I don't think my friends are stuffy," Penny argued hotly. "They happen to be interested in the same things I am. We get along fine. And I like working on the paper, or I wouldn't do it."

"Mike takes advantage of you," Pam insisted. "So does Bob Purcell, wishing half his work on you. But do any of them ever ask you for dates? Do you have any fun? Why, that crowd doesn't know it's alive. Bob thinks he's so intellectual and Maggie—"

"Pam, stop it!" Penny broke in. "Let's not fight. Bob's okay when you get to know him. And Maggie and I are good friends. As for Mike, if I'm satisfied with the way he treats me, you don't have to worry."

"He could have asked you to the Hop tonight," Pam argued. "He didn't ask me."

Penny glared at her. "He found out you were going with Spark, that's why."

"Did you tell him so?"

"Well yes," Penny admitted. "He asked me if you were already dated."

"Why didn't you go to work on him?" Pam demanded.

"If the conversation got that far, I should think you could have wangled an invitation out of him quite easily."

"Maybe I didn't want to," Penny said. "If I have to—to wangle invitations—" she broke off, hating the very sound of the word, then rushed on before Pam could say anything. "Besides, Mike said he was broke. He's looking for an after-school job."

"He is?" Pam's brows lifted a little in surprise.

"Yes," Penny said firmly, "although I don't see how he can handle one, in addition to everything else he does."

Pam said thoughtfully, "I guess his folks don't have too much money. They live in a sort of dumpy little house. Anyway," she went on, pursuing her own train of thought, "the Hop costs practically nothing. You should have got him to ask you. The trouble with you, Pen, is you aren't realistic. You must learn you can't just be aloof and wait for a boy to make all the advances. You have to lead him on without his knowing it."

Penny said angrily, "Will you stop telling me what I should do? That may be your system, but there's no reason it should work for me. We're two different people. Just because we happen to look alike doesn't mean we're the same inside. You use your methods and let me figure out things for myself!"

"Why, Penny!" Pam exclaimed, staring at her in surprise. "I do believe you're really mad. I was only trying to help."

"Well, don't!" Penny said flatly. But she felt herself cooling off a little. It was impossible to stay angry with Pam.

"It's just that I hate to think of you sticking around home brooding all evening." Pam's voice sounded troubled.

"Who's brooding?" Penny asked. "For that matter, who's sticking around home? Maggie and I are going to the movies."

"I suppose that's better than nothing," Pam said.

"It certainly is," Penny agreed, hopping down off the bed. "Maybe you wouldn't enjoy it, but Maggie and I expect to have fun."

Penny proceeded to get cleaned up, to change into her rust-colored jersey dress with the wide brown leather belt. Pam was still working on her hair when Penny called from the doorway, "Got to go now. Have fun."

"Oh, I will," Pam smiled at her. "You, too."

Penny nodded and went on out into the living room where Mother was arranging little white chrysanthemums in a luster bowl on the coffee table. Mother was wearing a gold-colored blouse and a slim black velveteen skirt. Her hair was brushed up from her ears to disclose tiny golden earrings shaped like shells. She looked quite youthful and very pretty.

Penny said, "The flowers are pretty and so are you."

"Well, thanks, dear," Mother smiled her pleasure at the compliment. "Lucius sent them. He's coming over tonight to play some bridge and bringing a friend with him."

"A man friend?" Penny asked teasingly.

Mother laughed a little. "Well, yes, I believe so."

"A double-date," Penny said, her voice confidentially low, "for you and Gran."

Mother's amused voice was low, too, so that Gran, dressing in her bedroom, wouldn't hear. "Probably," Mother confided, "he'll be around seventy. Most of Lucius' friends are, I've found. But I won't mind, so long as he plays decent bridge."

Penny shrugged into her coat and caught up her gloves and wallet as the doorbell chimed. "That'll be Maggie."

Mother told her to have a good time and Penny ran lightly down to join her friend at the front door.

"Hi," she greeted Maggie, "you're right on time."

"So are you," Maggie said, as they moved down the walk.

There was a sign on the lawn that read HOWARD HOUSE—INTERIOR DECORATION. The front of the house was skillfully floodlighted, so that it stood out clearly against the night, like a stage setting. Penny was so used to the sign and the floodlight, she wasn't consciously aware of them at all.

Just as she and Maggie reached the sidewalk, however, there was a brisk pattering of applause and a male voice startled them, saying, "You look like a couple of leading ladies, making your entrance in the first act. I couldn't resist giving you a hand."

Bob Purcell's scratchy dry voice identified him to both girls, even before they could make out his lanky outline clearly in the darkness.

"Bob, you goon!" Maggie said. "You scared us."

"Sorry," Bob chuckled, falling into step with them. "Where you two heading?"

"The movies," Penny said.

Bob drawled, "By the strangest coincidence, that's my destination, too."

"You mean you're not going to the Hop?" Maggie asked in mock horror.

"Please," Bob said. "Dancing is not one of my outstanding accomplishments. And I refuse to indulge in activities in which I cannot excel."

They walked along together, the three of them, kidding and laughing, till they reached the theater. There stood Mike in the bright Neon glow. Penny's heart leaped. Bob hadn't said a word about meeting Mike.

Yet Mike was saying to him, "You're late, character." He addressed himself then to Penny and Maggie, "What did you do to detain him. Come on now, confess."

"We're innocent, so help us," Penny said.

And Maggie added, "He attached himself to us like a leech. We couldn't escape him."

Bob explained, with complete gravity, "I was just passing Penny's house when they came out. Naturally my ingrained chivalry rose up and refused to let me slink off and leave them to walk all alone through the jungle darkness. Who knows what dangers threatened these two fair flowers of American womanhood—"

"Okay, okay," Mike laughed. "But let's get in now, shall we, before the main picture starts?"

He put a hand on the girls' shoulders to get them under way and he and Bob followed close behind. It was the most natural thing in the world for all of them to troop into the theater together, to find seats side by side. Fate seemed to be with Penny in that detail. Maggie edged in first, then Bob, then Penny and Mike. This was better than her dreams, Penny thought.

She had a hard time keeping her mind on the picture. It was so wonderful to sit there beside Mike, eating popcorn out of the same box, occasionally feeling their fingers touch accidentally. A sort of electric current seemed to pass through Penny when this happened, engendering a most agreeable little shock. If only it could have been happening to Mike, too. If only he might have reached

out, during the picture's more romantic moments, and
given her hand a little squeeze. But, of course, he didn't.
He only passed her the popcorn and spoke casually a few
times about some point in the picture. Still, warm thank-
fulness wrapped Penny about like a cloak, to think she
hadn't let Pam fix up a dance date for her. Then she'd
have missed this.

Of course, she reminded herself grimly, it was in no sense
a real date with Mike. It had just happened. But Mike
didn't seem bored, he acted as if he was enjoying himself.
Maybe, now that the ice had been broken, he would ask
her to go out with him sometime. At least on a double-
date with Maggie and Bob. Penny knew it was foolish to
let herself hope so hard, but she couldn't help it.

Afterward, Mike suggested that they stop at the Hangout for a soda. Penny's heart lifted still higher. He hadn't
had to do that at all. He *must* have wanted to. Not until
they reached the place and found it closed and dark did
realization strike them.

"Not a brain cell working!" Bob mourned. "We should
have known."

"But why?" Penny was the only one who didn't understand.

"It's never open on nights when there's a dance at
school," Maggie explained.

Mike looked at his wristwatch in the glow of a street
light. "It's after ten. The drugstores won't be open,
either."

"Come on over to my house," Maggie said, "if you'll
settle for hot chocolate and cookies."

"I'll settle for anything," Bob said. "I'm hungry."

Mike, too, was agreeable. So they walked the four

blocks to Maggie's house through the brisk cold night. The moon was bright above and when Penny glanced up, she saw that more stars than she could ever remember seeing were scattered across the sky.

Mike was looking up, too. He said, "When I was a kid, I used to study them. For a while I thought I wanted to be an astronomer. There's the Dipper. And there's Venus."

Penny's eyes followed his pointing finger. "They remind me of that poem by Stevenson about 'thousands of millions of stars.' "

"You like poetry?" Mike asked.

"Some," Penny admitted. "I like the kind that makes sense, so I can understand what the poet's talking about."

"Good girl!" Mike grinned. "You and I both. Some of this modern stuff's so obscure, I'll bet even the poet's confused."

Bob Purcell jumped into the conversation then in disagreement and Maggie took prompt exception to his views. The result was a four-way argument all the rest of the way to Maggie's house. Her parents proved to be in bed, but Maggie led the way to the cheerful rather old-fashioned kitchen. She and Penny made hot chocolate and got out cheese and crackers and cookies while the boys set the table. It was fun lingering over the food, talking and laughing and arguing, with Maggie warning them now and then not to get too noisy. Penny hated to have the evening end.

But eventually they realized it was time to break up. After whispered good nights and smothered laughter in the front hall, Penny and the two boys went outside together.

At the sidewalk, Bob said casually, "I'll take Penny home. It's right on my way."

And Mike, who lived in the opposite direction, agreed without a moment's hesitation, "Okay. It was fun. Be seeing you," and strode off with his long easy stride, his hands thrust deep into his pockets.

The taste of disappointment was bitter in Penny's throat. Darn it, she thought, why couldn't Mike have lived her way and Bob just the opposite? But no, fate was always dealing her low blows like that. Anyway, even with Bob taking her home, the evening had been almost as good as her dreams.

Chapter Ten

MOTHER GETS A BREAK

THE clear crisp early fall days merged into the muggy cold of November. Gran, who often quoted poetry, of which she knew a great variety of snatches, murmured feelingly, " 'The melancholy days are come, the saddest of the year—' "

But she didn't really mean it. The next minute she would be singing over the dishes, or laughing at something Celia or the twins had said. They were all very happy that fall. Both Gran and Celia had made friends in Glenhurst, just as Pam and Penny had. It was a friendly town and there were always a great many church and club activities afoot, as well as the more purely social doings. Chipper old Lucius Hancock came often to the house, as did other friends of Celia's and Gran's. As for the twins' friends, they were always stopping by, sure of a warm welcome. Boys and girls often gathered in the cheerful upper rooms of Howard House, to play games or records, or just to sit talking and laughing over the apparently inexhaustible bowls of popcorn and pitchers of hot chocolate Gran always seemed to supply so effortlessly.

Once Randy Kirkpatrick said, "This is a nice place to be, you know it?" He looked around the big informal room speculatively, as if he were trying to figure out why.

"There's something kind of warm and hospitable about the atmosphere."

Mike, who was sprawled low on the couch with his long legs thrust out before him, nodded. "Sure there is. That's why we hang around so much. It couldn't be the company."

"Take it back," Pam threatened, picking up a pillow, "or I'll bop you."

"Okay, okay," Mike grinned at her. "I'm too comfortable to fight."

He and Randy had dropped in unexpectedly that evening. They had arrived separately, half an hour or so apart. Now Pam sat on the couch between them, while Penny hunched cross-legged on the floor in front of the record player, going through stacks of albums. She was looking for an old Harry James recording that all of them had decided they wanted to hear. Somehow, although she was aware that both boys had stopped by to see Pam, Penny didn't feel awkward or ill at ease about it. Randy always treated her so agreeably and her friendship with Mike was so firmly established, there was no cause for self-consciousness. If she had given the matter a thought, Penny would simply have felt that she was one of a congenial group, as welcome as any of the others and quite as much at ease. The past few months had done that much to improve her mental attitude and give her a truer perspective.

Randy went on, pursuing his train of thought doggedly, "Sometimes houses almost seem to have personalities, just like people. This one's got a nice easy-going one."

"Yeah," Mike agreed, "it sure has. Some houses kind of make you feel like a louse if you spill popcorn or get a speck of mud on the floor or bump into a table. But not this one."

"Giving all the credit to the house," Pam said aggrievedly, "when actually it's the charming people who live in it!"

Penny chuckled. "I think he's hinting for popcorn."

"You're p-sositively p-sychic," Mike beamed at her.

"We'll have to pop it ourselves," Pam said, jumping up and slipping her hand into Randy's. "Gran's gone to the movies with Mr. Hancock and Mother's deep in balancing books for the month's end. Come on, Randy, you and I will pop corn. Mike, you help Penny find that record."

Thus, Penny thought wryly, might a queen bestow her favors. "Mike, stay with Penny. Randy, come help me." Another night it might be the other way around. And whichever one Pam invited to accompany her to the kitchen would go eagerly, gladly, just as Randy was going. And the one left with her would hide his disappointment, as Mike was hiding it.

"Oh, well," Penny thought philosophically, as Mike squatted down beside her on the floor and picked up an album, "Pam's giving me a break this time, even if she doesn't know it."

" 'Clair de Lune,' " Mike said, turning the pages of the album. "That's one of my favorites."

Penny glanced up at him in surprise. "Is it, Mike? I love it, too. Put it on, why don't you?"

"Okay," Mike grinned, getting up and putting the record on the turntable. "Set us to looking for Harry James, will they? We'll show 'em."

He proceeded to select a whole stack of classical records, Penny siding with and abetting him. Glorious music poured out into the room. Mike lay on his stomach at Penny's feet, his chin on his palm, his blue eyes dreaming. Neither of them said much. Words weren't necessary. The music seemed to weave a sort of spell about them, they simply listened and enjoyed it.

Penny thought wistfully, "We do like the same things. We're congenial in so many ways. Oh, Mike, if only you could realize we have a lot more in common than you and Pam. If only you felt about me as I feel about you—"

Pam came in from the kitchen then, with Randy at her heels bearing a big bowl of popcorn. "Well, isn't this cozy," she said. "Just a pair of long-hairs."

"Good music's wasted on you," Mike jeered.

But the way his face lit up at the sight of Pam made a knife twist in Penny's heart. . . .

One day shortly before the holidays, Pam and Penny came home from school to find Mother so swamped with customers that they both had to pitch in and help her. Business at Howard House had improved steadily, to the point where Celia was seriously considering hiring a full-time assistant. She had to do so much chasing back and forth on various jobs, with furnishings and bolts of drapery material loaded into the old station wagon Lucius Hancock had helped her procure, that she often had to call in Dorothea Crane to take care of the shop during her absence. Mrs. Crane had studied interior decoration before her marriage and now that her children were in school, she was quite willing to help Celia out whenever she was needed. In fact, she would have liked to work at Howard House every day. And Celia was eager to have her do so, as soon as she felt she could afford the additional expense.

This particular afternoon, it seemed to Penny that Mother was filled with a kind of restrained excitement. Her eyes were shining and her cheeks seemed pinker than usual. She continued to wait on customers with her usual agreeable competence, but all the time Penny had the feeling that Mother was anxious to have a moment alone with her and Pam in order to tell them something. Or was she just imagining that, Penny wondered, as she tried to hang onto her own patience and cope with a rather fluttery woman customer who couldn't make up her mind about table lamps? Penny noticed Pam casting an occasional inquiring look in Mother's direction, as if she, too, sensed something strange in her manner.

Not until the shop had cleared at closing time, did Mother get a chance to inform them, "I've got the most wonderful news! All afternoon I've been simply popping to tell you."

She rushed on to supply details. Randy Kirkpatrick's mother had stopped in at the shop earlier. She was, according to Celia, quite beautiful, stunningly mink-coated, and very pleasant.

"It's easy to see," Mother said, "where Randy gets his nice ways. Of course, his father may be perfectly agreeable, too, for all I know. But his mother's wonderful. So friendly and easy-mannered and not at all condescending." She had told Celia she'd been wanting to meet her, having heard so much about the twins and her from Randy.

"But I soon began to suspect that was only a ruse," Mother informed Pan and Penny, her blue eyes sparkling, a little smile quirking her mouth. "She was very interested in the shop and spent quite a bit of time browsing around and looking at everything, sort of appraising it and me, it seemed. Well, the upshot was, she asked if I undertook full scale jobs of decoration. And, of course, I said yes. So then—" Mother sounded quite breathless with wonder at the memory of what had happened next, "she asked me to come over tomorrow morning for a conference about doing over the whole downstairs of the Kirkpatrick house."

"That's wonderful!" Penny exclaimed.

And Pam echoed, "Wonderful! Why, they've got one of the most absolutely spectacular houses in Glenhurst."

"I know," Mother nodded, reaching out to give them both an enthusiastic hug. "There's a terrific amount of prestige to a job like that. If Mrs. Kirkpatrick likes my work—well, you can just imagine all the jobs it'll mean in the future."

"And more money," Pam added, beaming.

"You can get Mrs. Crane to help every day," Penny's eyes were alight, too.

All during dinner the Kirkpatrick job was the main topic of conversation. Gran, who had heard the good news before the twins got home from school, had prepared an especially nice meal by way of celebration.

Pam asked thoughtfully, over dessert, "Do you suppose Randy suggested the idea to his folks?" She reminded Penny, "You know how he was talking about our house one night upstairs, about how friendly it seemed, what a nice personality it had, as houses go? Maybe he got to talking that way to his mother, too."

"If he had any part in it, I'm glad," Celia said. "I suppose he might have mentioned me, if he knew they were thinking of having some re-decoration done. Anyway, it's the kind of break I've hoped for. The Kirkpatricks are important people in town; they have a lot of wealthy friends, some of whom may need their houses done over."

"Do you suppose," Pam asked with a little Mona-Lisa-ish smile, "Randy figured this might be a way to get in good with me?"

"Modesty," Gran snorted, "is certainly not one of your virtues, Pam."

"Well, I don't see why you say that," Pam objected. "I'm just being realistic. Randy's been pretty unhappy lately over my seeing so much of Spark. He just might have figured that this would be a good way to sort of make a favorable impression."

"So he persuades his family to spend all that money doing over their house," Gran said drily, "just to make a favorable impression on you? Really, Pam!"

"Money," Pam argued, "doesn't mean too much to the Kirkpatricks. And, as Mother said, they may have been figuring on having the work done. But Randy may very well have persuaded his mother to come to Howard House."

"If he did," Mother smiled, "I'm grateful. So long as I can suit the Kirkpatricks, I won't care how I happened to get the job."

"Anyway," Pam went on blissfully pursuing her own train of thought, "I'm glad she came to see you before Randy realized he doesn't have to worry about Spark any more."

"How come?" Penny asked, her attention arrested.

"Now that the football season's over," Pam admitted, "I've suddenly begun to realize that Spark's just a teensy

bit dull. I mean a girl can't go on simply panting with
vital interest over different methods of forward passing
and stuff like that. And there's no getting around the
fact that football is Spark's main topic of conversation."

"It always was," Penny couldn't resist reminding her.
If only it could have been Mike Pam had decided to scuttle.

"Better watch that," Pam said drily. "Your claws are
showing a little."

Mother spoke thoughtfully, and apparently she had been
pursuing her own train of thought as diligently as Pam
had. "Those English manor-type houses are usually rather
dark, so I suppose I'll have to keep the color scheme as
light as possible."

Penny opened her lips to answer Pam, then thought
better of it and closed them again. Maybe she had sounded
a little catty. After all, it was none of her affair if Pam
chose to drop Spark Mathews.

"Randy," Pam went on dreamily, "is really lots more
super than Spark. I think Spark's shoulders just sort of
bewitched me for a while."

"Where does Mike come in?" Penny asked, keeping her
voice quite casual and indifferent.

"On the other hand," Mother said, "the trend just now
is toward darker shades, especially for the walls. It's going
to be quite a stimulating problem to work on, but I'm
sure I can lick it."

"Of course you can," Gran said with staunch confidence.

"Mike?" Pam's eyes met Penny's. "Oh, he's pretty
super, too, when you get right down to it. If he just had
the convertible and all the money to spend on a girl that
Randy has—well, how irresistible can you get?"

Penny said, "I don't think that's very nice. After all, Mike can't help it because he doesn't have much money."

"And Randy," Pam admitted, "can't help it if he has."

"Mike's getting a job starting Monday," Penny told her.

"He is?" Pam asked interestedly. "Where?"

"At McKee and Dane's," Penny said, "as a stock man. He'll be working every day after school till Christmas, then just on Saturday. He was telling me about it this afternoon when I was doing some personals for the *Crier*."

"He *must* need money," Pam said. "McKee's stays open till nine o'clock every night till Christmas, don't they?"

Penny nodded. "All but Wednesdays. I guess you won't be seeing much of him for a while except at school."

"Oh, well," Pam shrugged. "I'll try to bear up."

"Those mullioned windows," Mother said consideringly, "have a certain old-world charm, but they're tough to drape. I wonder if hand-blocked linen—" her voice trailed off.

After a minute, Gran got to her feet. "Well, Pam, it's your turn to do the dishes."

"Oh, I can't!" Pam wailed. "Penny, will you be a perfect darling and switch with me? I forgot all about it being my turn tonight and Randy's coming by at seven so we can catch the early movie."

"Okay," Penny agreed.

She thought, "If it had been Mike she was going with, I might have objected to switching. But why should I put obstacles in her way if it's only Randy?"

A little smile pulled at her lips as she started stacking the dessert plates.

Chapter Eleven

THE SLEIGH RIDE

ECEMBER was a magic month, filled with rush and bustle. Penny had never been happier and Pam was caught up in her customary gay whirl of activity, boys calling up and dropping in, wonderful dates shaping up, fun and excitement. Penny had her share of things to do, too, and if they were less spectacular than Pam's activities, they were, nonetheless, satisfying to her and thoroughly absorbing.

Howard House swarmed with customers, necessitating Dorothea Crane's working there every day. Already Celia was knee-deep in the preliminaries of doing over the downstairs rooms in the Kirkpatrick's home. The actual work wouldn't be started until after the first of the year, but a great deal of planning was necessary, which entailed frequent conferences between Ellen Kirkpatrick and Celia. Sometimes these were held at the Kirkpatricks', sometimes at Howard House. Randy's mother was enthusiastic over Celia's ideas. The two women became very friendly during their endless discussions of color and fabrics and all the other angles that entered into a large-scale decorating job. During her visits at the Kirkpatricks', Celia also met Randy's father, Dolph Kirkpatrick, and Ellen's brother, Paul Gerard, who was staying with them for a while.

Neither Pam nor Penny gave too much thought to

Mother's job with the Kirkpatricks, other than to be glad she had got it and happy for her because it was working out so well. They were both busy with their own affairs. The rush of school work immediately prior to the Christmas vacation period filled the greater part of their days. Evenings there were countless things to do, skating on the frozen lake, school club activities, movies and dancing parties.

The Headlines Club sponsored a sleigh ride for its members one Wednesday night, with food and square dancing afterward in the school gym. Penny and Maggie Wright and Bob and Mike gravitated toward each other to form a casual sort of foursome. The night was cold, but clear and starry. Everyone was bundled to the eyebrows and scarcely felt the nip of the wind as they all snuggled down companionably into the roomy straw-filled sleigh. Up ahead the broad-beamed horses swung along rhythmically to the jingle of their sleigh bells. The crowd sang all the old songs and a lot of new ones, their voices ringing through the night, their breath puffing out in clouds along with the music. Feeling Mike's shoulder firm against hers as the sleigh lurched around a corner, Penny knew a wonderful kind of elation that grew out of being young and full of bright improbable dreams and capable of enjoying each new experience keenly and to the fullest extent. She sighed, a very small sigh of sheer pleasure.

"Cold?" Mike asked.

Penny was going to say, "No," but she changed it to, "Not very," as Mike's arm went around her.

It didn't mean a thing, Penny reminded herself sternly as her heart leaped. He was just holding her against him to keep her warm. He'd have done the same for Maggie

or any other girl he happened to be sitting next to. Penny
didn't suppose there was a boy in the whole sleigh who
didn't have his arm around someone. It was practically
unanimous. Sleigh rides were so wonderful!

She sat there, close to Mike, feeling warmth creep
through her, while talk and laughter and corny jokes
eddied about them. The voices made a sort of sweet music
in Penny's ears, combined with the jingling bells and the
crunch of snow under the sleigh's runners and the horses'
hooves. Mike's rather good baritone rang out, starting
the singing up again. Penny sang, too, along with the others, although she had only a vague idea of what she was
singing. She scarcely moved, there beside Mike, feeling
the pressure of his arm about her and wishing the ride
could last forever.

It didn't, of course. But back at Glen High there were
gaily decorated tables in the gym, stacked with sandwiches and doughnuts and quantities of hot punch. The
crowd gathered around them hungrily and the food melted
away. Then there was square dancing, with Mr. Norton,
the athletic director, doing the calling. Mr. Norton did
not look like his staid school-day self at all. He had on a
violently plaid shirt and a red neck-scarf. Even his voice
sounded different, raucously gay and devil-may-care,
shouting "Swing your partner!" and "Do-si-do!"

Penny danced with Mike and Bob and a boy named
Clark from her physics class. Then Mike again. She wasn't
terrifically in demand, but she wasn't a wall flower, either.
The realization filled her with new confidence.

"A happy medium, that's me," Penny thought, as she
danced the next number with Maggie. "But there are al-

ways more girls than boys at an affair like this, so I'm doing okay."

Penny had never had as much fun at a dance as she did that night at the Headlines' party. She tried to analyze her pleasure and realized that she wasn't worrying about her popularity the way she used to. She wasn't scanning each boy's face anxiously, with a desperate hope burning within her that he might be going to ask her to dance. She was infinitely more relaxed and easy than she had ever been at a party before. The crowd about her were friends; she liked them and they liked her. What was there to worry about and get into a dither over?

"The next one's a Virginia Reel," Bob Purcell's dry voice said in her ear. "I reel like nobody's business. How about it, Penny?"

She nodded, smiling. "Okay, Bob."

Moving through the intricacies of the dance, with Bob's hand tight on hers and Mr. Norton's brisk voice calling, "Bow to your partner" and "Promenade all!" Penny thought, "Quite a whirl I'm having—in more ways than one." And her smile was so vivid and her eyes so bright that Mike Bradley, looking down into her face as the dance whirled them momentarily together, was startled by her complete resemblance to Pam. Just then it would have been quite impossible, even for anyone who knew them as well as he did, to tell them apart.

Pam, who had had a date with Randy that night, got in just a few minutes after Penny did. Penny hadn't made a move yet to get undressed. She was sitting on the edge of her bed, her feet thrust out before her, a little reminiscent smile curving her mouth.

She said, "Pam, it was the most absolutely terrific evening! I can't ever remember having so much fun!"

"Well, good, baby," Pam said agreeably. "A sleigh ride and square dance doesn't exactly send me—but everybody to his own notion." She went on then before Penny could answer, "Randy and I had fun, too. After the movies he took me out to the country club for something to eat. I just love it there!"

Listening with less than half an ear as Pam proceeded to describe her evening at length and in detail, Penny thought, "I don't care how gorgeous the country club is, or how swanky the crowd. I'd rather spend my evening exactly as I did."

The memory of Mike's arm, firm and hard around her in the sleigh, and of the way he had laughed down at her while they were dancing, made a warm glow in Penny's heart. Tonight he hadn't seemed to mind that she wasn't Pam. In fact, he'd scarcely seemed to notice. And he had brought her home, despite the fact that Bob Purcell wouldn't have had to go a step out of his way to do so. If this realization had occurred to Mike, he hadn't mentioned it. Neither, thank goodness, had Bob, who had seemed to be enjoying himself thoroughly, in his own sardonic way, in Maggie's company.

"Hey!" Pam squeezed Penny's shoulder, snapping her back to the present. "I don't believe you heard a word I said."

"I did, too," Penny assured her. "You went to the movies and afterward Randy took you to the country club."

"And what else?" Pam demanded.

"What—else?" Penny repeated. "Was there more?"

"I knew you weren't listening," there was a trace of

exasperation in Pam's manner. "Penny, this could be serious. Pay attention now and stop daydreaming. I've been
telling you Randy's parents were at the club—and his
uncle." Pam's voice underlined the last words portentously. At Penny's blank look, she reminded, "You've heard
Mother mention his uncle, Paul Gerard?"

Penny nodded, still mystified, and Pam went on, lower-
ing her tone confidentially, "Mother didn't tell us he was
absolutely one of the most attractive men you ever saw.
Older men, that is. He's sort of a combination Ronald
Colman and Gregory Peck with maybe just a dash of Clark
Gable. Very suave and sort of debonaire. And you know
what he is? A foreign newspaper correspondent—only he's
taking a leave of absence because of being sort of worn
down by all his harrowing experiences. And all Mother
told us was that he was a newspaper man! Can you
imagine?"

"Well, but—isn't he a newspaper man?" Penny asked
doubtfully. "I don't see—"

"You will," Pam went on grimly, "if you'll just wait
till I finish. The thing is, Penny, he kept asking me questions about Mother. He pumped me absolutely dry! I
mean, there was no detail too small to interest him vitally.
I think," she added ominously, "he's falling in love with
her."

"But—" Penny objected faintly, "Mother hasn't said
much about him at all!"

"She has and she hasn't," Pam insisted. "She's really
mentioned him quite a lot, along with Randy's parents. I
mean, she hasn't exactly singled him out to talk about. But,
in a way, I guess that isn't so good."

"It isn't?" Penny asked doubtfully. There was a strange

heaviness in her chest at the thought of Mother actually getting interested in a man, even Randy's attractive bachelor uncle. "How do you mean, Pam?"

"Well," Pam elaborated, "if she really is as intrigued with him as he seems to be with her, she just might feel she'd rather we didn't know about it yet. Maybe she wants to wait till he asks her to marry him before she confides in us."

Penny supposed it could be like that. On the other hand—

She objected, "But, Pam if she's not specially interested in him, that's the way she'd act, too. I mean, maybe her not talking about him simply means he's not important to her."

"I hope you're right," Pam said with a little sigh, "but I don't think so. I have a feeling—" she broke off to lay one hand dramatically over her heart, "here. Honestly, the way he wanted to hear every little detail about Mother —and he's so perfectly fascinating! It's easy enough for you to be philosophical about the situation, but you haven't seen him yet and I have. Actually, I don't see how any woman could resist him."

"Even Mother?" Penny asked anxiously. "You know we got pretty worried about that man she worked with in the city—"

"Him!" Pam sniffed. "Why, he was fat! And beginning to get bald, too. Mother wouldn't even be tempted by the thought of marrying him—"

"Marrying?" Penny repeated, staring at Pam. "Aren't you rushing things a little?"

"Well, it's a possibility," Pam pointed out. "There's no use burying our heads in the sand."

"No, but—" Penny began, when the door of their bedroom swung open and Mother stood there on the threshold in her coral flannel robe, her hair tousled and her eyes sleepy looking.

"What are you two talking about?" she asked, her voice low so as not to disturb Gran. She added then, with a little smile, "It's pretty late for such long drawn-out conversation."

"We didn't mean to wake you," Pam told her, while Penny felt warm embarrassed color creep across her face. "We were just talking about our dates—stuff like that."

"Did you both have fun?" Mother asked, struggling with a yawn.

"Oh, yes," Penny told her. "I had a wonderful time. Mike brought me home."

"He did?" There was a faint note of surprise in Pam's tone, in the lift of her eyebrows. "You didn't tell me that."

"You didn't give me a chance," Penny grinned at her. "You were so intent on telling me about your evening with Randy and about seeing his folks at the country club and all."

Pam's gray glance rested on Mother's face as she added, "I met his uncle, too. The one you mentioned."

"Oh, yes," Mother nodded, smiling, "Paul."

First names already, Pam's glance said plainly to Penny. Aloud she said. "He's so attractive. Why didn't you tell us he was simply out of this world?"

Mother chuckled, then yawned again. "I should have thought, at your age, you'd have found him one-foot-in-the-graveish. He's well over forty."

"So are a lot of perfectly fascinating men," Pam argued.

Mother stared at her. "Don't tell me, darling, that you've developed a crush on a man old enough to be your father. Paul Gerard's a charming person, but his nephew's much more suitable for you."

Pam said with dignity, "I haven't any crush on anybody. I simply pointed out that Randy's uncle is very attractive and that I didn't see why you'd never thought to tell us so."

"Oh," Mother said, "is that all you meant? Then I must apologize for the oversight. The truth is, I've had so many other details on my mind when I'm at the Kirkpatricks, maybe I haven't paid enough attention to Paul."

"He seemed quite interested in you," Pam said pointedly.

Mother patted her shoulder, smiling. "I hope you gave me a good reference, dear. And now you two simply have to quit talking and go to sleep. It's late."

Quite a while after they had got into bed, Pam spoke to Penny in the dark. "I wonder," she asked thoughtfully, "how it would be to have a stepfather?"

Penny objected sleepily, "Mother didn't sound a bit like she was falling in love. I don't see why you're so worried."

"You didn't see Paul Gerard," Pam said.

"Anyway," Penny spoke firmly, "Mother's a grown-up woman. She has a perfect right to remarry if she wants to."

"I suppose so," Pam said, after a long considering moment. "Just the same, I'm glad he'll be leaving Glenhurst in a month or so. Middle-aged romances usually take longer than that to get anywhere, I imagine."

Penny thought wryly, "Sometimes young ones do, too."

But it seemed to her that some progress had been made tonight.

Chapter Twelve

PENNY PLANS A PARTY

$\mathcal{E}$ACH year on New Year's Eve a big formal dance was held at the Glenhurst Country Club. Randy had invited Pam to it well in advance of the date, lest she make other plans for the evening. Had he but known it, Pam had been figuring on attending the dance with him ever since she first learned of it. The possibility that he might not ask her simply didn't cross her mind.

For such a very special occasion a new formal seemed indicated. When Pam broached the subject, Mother asked, "How would you like one as a Christmas gift from Gran and me?" Her smiling glance went to Gran's face for the confirmation she knew she'd find there.

"That would be perfect," Pam breathed. "Absolutely perfect!"

So Pam chose material and a pattern, with Mother paying the bill, and Gran made the dress. The result of her inspired efforts was a breathtakingly lovely concoction of palest yellow net and taffeta, with a boned strapless bodice and an incredible swirl of skirt.

Seeing it, Penny was almost sorry she had declined, when Gran and Mother offered her a new formal for Christmas, too. She had chosen instead a street-length dress in a soft copper-colored velveteen with marching gold buttons. But it, too, turned out quite beautifully in Gran's expert hands. And there wouldn't have been much sense in getting a formal when she wasn't going to the dance.

"Randy probably could have lined up a date for you," Pam reminded her, "if you had let me ask him. But you're so persnickety about things like that lately."

"You'd feel the same way," Penny told her, "if it was a question of my having to get a date for you."

"But what will you do New Year's?" Pam asked, her gray glance troubled. "It's only a couple of weeks off."

"I'll do something," Penny assured her, with more confidence than she felt. "Don't worry about me."

There was fresh snow for Christmas. It began to fall on Christmas Eve, so that when the twins and Mother and Gran came out of the candlelight service at church, the soft white flakes were swirling and blowing, cold and refreshing on their faces. The next day passed in a gay confusion of gifts and Christmas calls, of friends and neighbors dropping in. The Howards' living room was cozy with a blazing log fire on the hearth, with the enticing scent of Scotch pine, with talk and laughter and Christmas carols on the record player. Lucius Hancock lingered most of the day, having been invited to dinner. Paul Gerard stopped in briefly, so that Celia had a chance to thank him in person for the lovely red roses that he had sent her. Other friends of Mother's and Gran's stopped by, as did many young people. Maggie Wright and Jean Dickey and Susan Farnsworth, Randy and Mike and Spark Mathews and Bob Purcell—so many others Penny could scarcely keep track of them.

Switching off the tree-lights late that night, Celia said, "It's been a wonderful day, hasn't it?"

And Gran added, "This is the sort of friendliness I missed so in the city. Thank goodness, we moved away before I began to believe the wells of human kindness had dried up entirely."

Mother stood for a moment, a little smile pulling at her mouth. Then she chuckled. "Guess what! Paul Gerard invited me to the country club dance."

"He did?" Pam exclaimed. Her voice sounded just a little sharp.

"Well, that's nice," Gran said. "I hope you told him you'd go."

Penny didn't say anything for a minute. She was observing how young and sort of filled with wistful anticipation Mother's face looked. Why, Mother wasn't old enough to not have any dates and fun any more, to simply work all the time. It wasn't fair to expect she'd be satisfied with a life like that.

Penny said firmly, "I hope you said you'd go, too."

Pam flashed a warning glance at her, but Penny ignored it. Just because Mother went to a dance with Paul Gerard needn't necessarily mean she was planning to marry him. There was no point in Pam's getting into a tizzy over it.

Pam spoke doubtfully. "Wouldn't you feel a little out of place? I mean, both of you? The crowd'll probably be quite a bit younger."

Celia smiled. "Oh, I don't know. Paul says the Kirkpatricks and lots of their friends will be there. Maybe I won't seem too ancient."

Gran snorted, "That's silly. What a way to talk, Pam!"

"Oh, I didn't mean you were really old, Mother," Pam amended hastily. "But it's been so long since you've gone to a dance—"

"I think I still remember how to act," Mother told her.

"What will you wear?" Penny asked interestedly.

"My black dinner dress is perfectly good," Celia said, "and quite new so far as Glenhurst's concerned. It should do nicely. But I didn't actually tell Paul I'd go yet. I said I'd let him know."

"But why—" Penny began. And then she stopped abruptly.

The troubled way Mother was looking at her made the reason for her hesitation painfully clear. Penny thought starkly, "She's worried about me. She knows Pam's got a date. And now she herself has a chance for one. But I'm the problem. She doesn't want to leave me out in the cold."

Aloud Penny told Mother, "Don't hesitate on my account. Just this afternoon I had a wonderful idea about what I'd like to do New Year's Eve. I hadn't got around to asking you yet, the place has been so full of people today, but I thought it would be lots of fun if I could have some kids over that night. Not a big party, or anything. Just four or five people maybe. Maggie and Jean and—oh, maybe Bob and a couple more boys to sort of even it off. I haven't had time to put much thought on it yet, but if you wouldn't care—" She certainly hadn't had time to put much thought on it, Penny reflected wryly. The whole idea had popped, full-fledged, into her mind just that minute. It had been born of her desperate need to think of something, so that Mother wouldn't feel she'd have to stay home on her account.

Mother said, "Why, no, dear, I wouldn't care. If it's all right with Gran."

"Of course, it's all right," Gran said staunchly.

Her bright blue eyes met Penny's in a very knowing way. Did Gran see through her ruse, Penny wondered? Oh, well, what did it matter, so long as she went along with the idea so agreeably? Good old Gran. Penny slipped her arm around the plump shoulders to give her a big hug.

Gran said, "Leave the refreshments to me. You just keep 'em amused and occupied and I'll feed 'em."

So that was settled. Mother would accept Paul Gerard's invitation and Penny would invite some people over. She hoped Maggie and Jean could come and that they'd have some bright ideas about who else to invite. This was going to be pretty short notice for a New Year's Eve party, even a small one. She'd just have to do the best she could to work it out.

Getting ready for bed that night, Pam accused Penny, "You certainly didn't back me up very well. What are you trying to do, throw Mother and Randy's uncle together?"

"No," Penny said, "but Mother's got a right to have a little fun."

"Well, of course," Pam agreed. "But you saw for yourself today how attractive Paul Gerard is. Don't you think it would be simply playing with dynamite for Mother to see too much of him?"

"Maybe," Penny argued, "but that's for Mother to decide, isn't it?"

Pam snorted. "I get so mad at you sometimes. You just won't look at things realistically. Do you realize if Mother married him, he'd want her to go away somewhere with him when he starts working again? New York, Paris, anywhere!"

"Mother simply wouldn't desert us," Penny said, climbing into bed and snuggling her cheek down against the cool pillow.

"Well, she certainly couldn't take us along. It would just be a mess anyway you look at it."

"I'm too sleepy to look at it tonight," Penny said.

But a small qualm of uneasiness stirred in her. What Pam said made sense. It wouldn't be an easy problem to work out, if Mother should decide to marry Paul Gerard. And there was no denying that he was handsome. The gray hair at his temples gave him a look of worldliness and distinction, a look that was augmented by his rather sardonic smile. Anyway, Penny reminded herself as Pam switched off the light and got into bed, still kicking the subject of Mother and Paul Gerard around, it was certainly up to Mother to decide.

"All you have to decide," she told herself just before she dropped off to sleep, "is how to get a New Year's party put together in less than a week. . . ."

As a matter of fact, it didn't prove nearly so hard as Penny had feared. A few phone calls the next morning established the fact that she wasn't the only one who had been in danger of not having anything to do New Year's Eve.

Maggie exclaimed, "Why, Penny, that's a grand idea! Of course, I'll come. Want me to ask Bob? We're going skating this afternoon. I'm pretty sure he can make it New Year's."

So that took care of two guests.

Jean Dickey also accepted Penny's invitation with enthusiasm. When Penny asked her if she knew of any more boys they could get, Jean answered thoughtfully, "Shall I sort of feel out Curt Watson? He lives next door to me, only he's been away at college. He's just a freshman, though, so he wouldn't be too old. He was griping the other day because there wasn't much to do around here. He'd probably be tickled pink to go to a party."

The thing seemed to snowball under Penny's very eyes. She ran into Jerry Clark from her physics class that afternoon when she and Jean were playing table-tennis at the Park House. His brother Bill was with him and both boys were so friendly, playing doubles with Penny and Jean and giving them pointers on their backhand, that Penny felt emboldened to bring up the subject of New Year's Eve. And, sure enough, neither of them had anything planned. They'd be glad to come to her little party.

That night as Jean and Penny talked on the phone, Jean reminded her, "Now you've got four boys and only three girls."

"I know," Penny admitted. "It never seems to come out even. But Gran says any number up to ten or so is okay with her. So that gives me a little leeway."

Penny couldn't help a wistful wish that it had been the other way around. If she had an extra girl, instead of an extra boy, she might have got up the courage to invite Mike Bradley. Of course, he could have something else planned for New Year's Eve. Penny didn't know. Except for a little while on Christmas, she hadn't seen or heard from Mike since the beginning of the school holiday the previous week. And outside of their encounters at school, she hadn't seen much of him for the week or so before that. Mike's part-time job had been keeping him busy until nine o'clock at night when McKee and Dane's Department store closed. So Penny hadn't even had the bitter-sweet pleasure of seeing him briefly when he came over to take Pam out.

Jean's voice at the other end of the telephone wire brought her gradually back to the present. "There's Cindy Wentworth," Jean was saying. "You might try her. She's lots of fun."

"That's a good idea," Penny agreed. "I'll call her up right away."

But when she got Cindy on the phone, a further complication developed.

"Gee, Penny," Cindy said, "I'd love to come. I've been wondering what to do New Year's. But—" her voice quavered a little with anxiety, "Betty March and I were talking this afternoon and we agreed to do something together. You couldn't," she asked hopefully, "use another girl, could you?"

"Why—yes," Penny said rather breathlessly. "Yes, as a matter of fact, I could." Why, it was almost like Fate pulling the strings, she thought. Now she would need an extra boy. She could ask Mike—and keep her fingers crossed hoping he'd be able to come, that he'd want to.

"Oh, wonderful!" Cindy exclaimed enthusiastically. "I know Betty'll just love it, too. Thanks a million, Penny. . . ."

So that, Penny thought, hanging up slowly, was that. She wondered whether Pam would know anything about Mike's plans for New Year's Eve. Asking would be the only way to find out.

Penny went into the bedroom, where Pam was brushing her hair into a soft dark cloud before the dressing-table mirror. "Who were you phoning?" Pam asked curiously.

Penny told her. She told her, too, about Betty March.

"Now I've got an extra girl," she said, "where before it was an extra boy. Honestly!"

"Let's see," Pam pursed her lips thoughtfully, "who else could you ask?"

"How about Mike?" Penny suggested quickly. "You—don't happen to know what he's planning, do you?"

"Mike?" Pam's brows lifted a little. "He's been such a stranger lately. I wouldn't know."

"Well, he's been working," Penny reminded. "He didn't have much time for dates till just this week."

"So he keeps telling me," Pam chuckled. "So finally I relented and let him talk me into going to the movies with him tonight. You want me to ask him about New Year's for you?"

Penny shook her head. "No, thanks. I'll ask him myself when he comes."

The doorbell rang just then and Pam said, "That must be him now. Go down and let him in, why don't you, and then you'll have a good chance to invite him to your little party."

The superior way Pam said "your little party" made Penny half-angry. She didn't have to sound quite so condescending, even if she was going to a dance at the country club.

"Hi, Mike," Penny said, as she opened the door.

"Oh—hi," Mike said, with a little chuckle. "You know, for just a sec, I thought you were Pam."

"Well, I'm not," Penny said flatly. Maybe it was the lingering heat of her annoyance with Pam that lent her courage. She asked, "Are you all tied up New Year's Eve, Mike, or would you care to come over to a sort of party I'm having? Nothing elaborate," she went on, moved by the need to put all her cards on the table, "just some kids coming over. Jean and Maggie and Bob and a few others."

"Sort of fugitives from the rarified atmosphere your sister's going to breathe out at the country club?" Mike asked, grinning down at her.

Penny thought there was a slightly bitter twist to his grin. Apparently he had asked Pam to do something with him New Year's Eve—and had been disappointed.

"Something like that, I guess," Penny admitted, smiling, too. "We'll have fun, though," she added firmly.

"Sure, we will," Mike said, laying a big hand on her shoulder in friendly fashion. "Thanks for asking me."

Penny's heart lifted like a runaway elevator.

Chapter Thirteen

A WORD OF ADVICE

$\mathcal{H}$OLIDAY week flew past.
The weather was terrible, slush and sleet and raw pene-
trating wind, under a sky the color of gray slate. But
Penny was so busy she scarcely noticed the weather. And
Pam was even busier. Pam went to parties, she had dates
almost every night with one boy or another. Penny's activities were less exciting, a hen luncheon party at Maggie's,
the movies one night with Bob Purcell and Jean Dickey and
her next door neighbor, Curt Watson. Penny had endless
conferences with Gran over refreshments for the party,
with Maggie and Jean about things to do New Year's Eve
to keep the fun rolling along. This would be the first party
she had ever given without Pam's co-operation and Penny
was understandably anxious about its success.

One afternoon she stopped in the drugstore to have a
Coke between errands. Mike's voice hailed her from a
booth. As always, Penny's heart hurried a little faster at
his nearness.

"Why—hi, Mike," she answered.

"Come on, join me," Mike motioned toward the empty
bench opposite him. "I am feeling lower than an angle
worm's stomach at the moment. Maybe human compan-
ionship will help."

Sitting down at the narrow table, Penny's knees bumped

against Mike's. She had brought her own Coke over from the fountain and now she took a few thoughtful sips, her gray glance on Mike's face. "Why are you so low?" she asked.

"Hah!" Mike's laugh was hollow. "Funny you should ask me that. My despondence is directly due and traceable to your charming sister."

"Oh," Penny said. Then, after a moment's pause, "Did you—have a fight?"

Mike shook his head in the negative. "Nothing so definite as that. In a way, I wish we had. A good battle sometimes clears the air and resolves a lot of grievances. But, no, Pam and I are on as good terms as we ever were—I guess. It's just—" Mike's voice grew more troubled, "well, it's so hard to know where you stand with a girl like Pam. I mean there are so many guys hanging around her all the time, you sort of get lost in the shuffle."

Penny nodded. That was the way it was, all right. That was exactly the way Pam wanted it, too.

"She seems," Mike went on in a brooding sort of tone, "to figure that if one boy friend's a good thing, ten boy friends are ten times as good. The competition's rugged. I never saw a girl like her." He eyed Penny gravely for a minute. "You're not like her a bit, are you, Penny? Inside, I mean."

"I guess not," Penny murmured.

"She wraps you around her finger, too," Mike said. "Look at the way you do half her homework, lug books home all the time for both of you. Look at the way she risked getting you into a bad jam that time in trig."

"I just help her with homework," Penny defended Pam

automatically. "And that trig deal well, we never intend to pull anything like that again."

"*You* never intend to," Mike corrected.

But Penny shook her head. "No, Mike, Pam promised she'd never ask me to, either."

"Boy, you're sure loyal to her," Mike grinned crookedly.

"Well, naturally," Penny said. "After all, we're sisters, twin sisters. But—" suddenly she felt a need to confide in Mike, as he had been confiding in her. She went on seriously, her eyes wide and candid on Mike's face, "I haven't been just drifting along in Pam's trail lately. I've been striking out for myself more, not being such a carbon copy." She admitted, twisting her Coke glass around and around in her fingers, making the cracked ice tinkle, "It used to be, I'd try every way I knew to imitate Pam, to be exactly like her. But lately I've come to see that just because we look alike, it doesn't mean we're anything alike inside. So I'm trying to be me, Penny. That's why I go to Headlines Club and work on the paper. Pam thinks it's silly, but I like it. And I've been making my own friends, or trying to—not just drifting along in Pam's crowd, put up with because I'm her sister. It—hasn't been too easy, but I think it's worth while."

Suddenly, Penny realized that this was probably the longest, certainly the most revealing, speech she had ever made to a boy in her whole life. She felt embarrassment creep over her, felt herself flush. Her voice cracked a little, saying, "I—can't think why I'm burdening you with all this—"

"Why not?" Mike's voice was as steady as his blue eyes on hers. He reached over and laid his hand briefly, warmly over Penny's hand where it clung to the black marble edge of the table. "Why shouldn't you unburden yourself to me? We're friends, aren't we? And I've certainly been spilling my troubles to you."

Penny seemed to feel the pressure of his hand lingering on hers even after he had released it. She murmured, "I've —never talked like this with anyone before, any boy, that is."

"Then it's time you got started," Mike grinned. "As they say, confession's good for the soul. But to get back to Pam, it looks as if she's at the root of both your problems and mine. I guess," Mike said in a philosophical sort of tone, "I shouldn't complain, though. I'm not the only guy she's got going around in circles."

Penny nodded. There was no question about that.

"Randy," Mike enumerated, "Spark and me." His glance questioned Penny. "Wouldn't you say that right now we're the three she sees the most of?"

"Not Spark anymore," Penny said. "He's getting edged out by Joe Henderson."

"Neck-and-neck at the straightaway?" Mike asked wryly. "Sounds like a horse race. Would you say I'm getting edged out by Randy Kirkpatrick?"

"No," Penny said quickly, "I wouldn't say that, Mike. I'm sure Pam likes you, too."

Mike shook his head. "Sometimes I wonder."

"She wouldn't bother with you if she didn't." Penny knew Pam well enough to be sure of that.

Now it was Mike's turn to twist his Coke glass, to stare down thoughtfully into its icy depths. "It's kind of funny in a way," he admitted. "Randy's been able right along to give her a bigger whirl. on account of having the car and more money to spend. Not that I mean that's all she sees in him," he amended quickly, his eyes coming up to meet Penny's. "Randy's a good guy aside from that. But anyway," Mike's chuckle sounded just a shade bitter, "it's kind of ironic. I get myself a job so I'll have some money to throw around, too. So what happens? I had to work so late till Christmas, it gave Randy and Joe and Spark and the rest a clear track. Now that I only work on Saturdays, I can ask Pam for a date. But does she understand, as I'll bet you'd understand, Penny? Not on your life. She's riled at me because I've been quote neglecting her unquote."

He sounded so unhappy, Penny had to say something comforting. "Oh, Mike, I don't think she's really riled. She went out with you one night this week, didn't she?"

"Yeah," Mike nodded. "One measley date we've had since I finished working nights. So here I am, with plenty of lettuce and no girl to spend it on. How do you like that?"

Penny said, "She'll get over it. This week's been pretty busy. And of course Randy asked her to the dance New Year's 'way in advance."

"Yeah," Mike said, "I know. I had all that explained to me very sweetly in words of one syllable by your sister."

"But it's true, Mike," Penny told him earnestly. "Pam wasn't just giving you a run-around." She was feeling just then the pull of two loyalties, one to Pam, which was very familiar, and a newer one, amazingly strong, to Mike, whom she liked so well. Frowning, Penny thought, it couldn't be too unfair to Pam if she gave Mike just a teensy steer in the right direction. Almost of their own volition, her lips began to move, saying, "There's—just one thing,

Mike, if you wouldn't mind my giving you a word of advice."

"Boy, I need it," Mike said. "Shoot."

"It's funny with Pam," Penny's voice was low and just a little unsteady, "but I've seen it happen so often, I'm sure it's the case. Pam—seems to sort of lose interest in a boy if she feels—fairly sure of him. It hasn't happened yet with Randy, because, as you said, he's able to give her such a terrific whirl. But—she was very interested in you right at first, Mike, when she wasn't sure you were interested in her."

Mike stared at Penny for a moment. Then he said slowly, "That's right. She did act then as if I was something pretty special."

"It's always like that," Penny said faintly. "Then, when she can tell someone really likes her a lot—" her voice ran down miserably. It wasn't easy to tell Mike these things about Pam, even though she felt he was entitled to know them. But Mike had seemed so sunk and unhappy, she hadn't been able to stop herself. Well, now he knew. She'd done all she could for him.

She made a little move to get up, but Mike caught her hand, stopping her. "Wait a minute," he said. "I want to get this straight. When I was hard-to-get, Pam wanted me. Now she's got me, she's hard-to-get. Is that the way it works?"

Penny nodded. "I—have to go now, Mike. Really."

"I'm going, too," Mike said, getting up as Penny did. "I'll go with you."

"I've got lots of little errands," Penny warned. "I have to stop at the dime store and McKee's."

"I've got plenty of time," Mike said. "And I'm a good package carrier."

Walking down the street, he said thoughtfully, "Gee whiz, a guy would have to have a hole in his head to go to all that bother over a girl—even Pam."

Penny murmured, "I shouldn't have told you all that. I've never talked to anyone else that way." She caught her lip hard between her teeth.

Mike slipped his hand under her arm and squeezed it gratefully. "Don't feel bad about it, Penny. Believe me, I appreciate your help." He shook his bare blond head ruefully. "When a guy gets a girl under his skin the way I've got your sister, it warps his judgment."

"You really like her a lot, don't you, Mike?" Penny asked huskily.

"That," Mike said, "is the understatement of the year."

In a way, Penny felt better, but in another way, she felt much worse. It was a relief to know she hadn't undermined Mike's feeling for Pam. But there was a deep pain within her at the realization of just how terrific that feeling was. . . .

On New Year's Eve all was rush and confusion at the Howards'. Everyone was getting dressed at once and all of them managed to get in each other's way. Randy and his uncle Paul came by for Pam and Mother fairly early, to carry them off to the Kirkpatricks', where a crowd of friends were assembling before the dance. Mother looked more beautiful in her long black dress, with the white orchids Paul had sent, than Penny could ever remember having seen her. And Pam, of course, was absolutely devastating in her new yellow formal, with a black velvet ribbon around her throat and tiny black velvet gloves and Randy's wrist corsage of yellow rosebuds. Penny breathed a small sigh of relief to have her out of the house before her own guests, particularly Mike, arrived.

Gran heard the sigh and misinterpreted it. She murmured, her arm around Penny's shoulder as the downstairs door closed on the sound of departing voices, "First dance you want to go to, honey, I'll make you just as pretty a dress."

"There's nothing wrong with this one," Penny said gratefully, smoothing the copper-colored velveteen over her slim hips. "I just love it, Gran."

"You look mighty pretty," Gran told her.

"So do you," Penny said.

And Gran went bustling off toward the kitchen in her good maroon crepe, with a little organdy party apron tied on over it for protection. "Flatterer!" she chuckled.

A few minutes later, Lucius Hancock arrived. "Hello, Penny, or Pam, as the case may be," he boomed cordially as Penny let him in.

"I'm Penny," she told him, smiling, and led the way upstairs, where she put his hat and coat away in the closet.

"You don't mind my coming over to lend your grandmother moral support and also help her serve the refreshments?" Lucius asked earnestly.

"Of course not," Penny told him. "I'm glad to have you."

"Thank you, my dear," he said. "New Year's Eve is a singularly dismal occasion to spend alone."

Penny's pitying glance followed his erect back as he headed toward the kitchen. In honor of this special occasion, Lucius was wearing a white shirt and neat pinstriped dark suit, quite at variance with his customary casual sport clothes. A little amused smile twisted Penny's lips. He was kind of cute when you got right down to it. And so was Gran. They were probably going to enjoy her party as much as any of the younger guests.

The bell rang again and Penny's friends began arriving so quickly that she was kept busy letting them in. When Mike came, he was carrying a small oblong florist's box, which he presented to Penny with a flourish.

"Why, Mike!" Penny exclaimed in pleased astonishment when she had opened it to discover two creamy gardenias nestling inside. "You needn't have brought me a corsage— but it's beautiful!"

"Glad you like it," Mike dismissed her thanks largely.

Soon the crowd was all assembled and the fun began. Penny and Maggie between them had figured out enough games to keep things from slowing down. In between they played records and danced a little. Gran and Lucius presided over the delicious buffet supper like a pair of amiable genii, bringing in reinforcements of sandwiches and cake and soft drinks whenever the original supply looked a little depleted. At midnight there was a raucous tooting of horns and bursting of balloons. Everyone, including Gran and Lucius, locked arms in a big circle and sang "Auld Lang Syne." "Happy New Year, Happy New Year," everyone exclaimed to everyone else.

Nor did the gayety run down then. More games were played. More records listened to and danced to. By the time the last guest had departed, after telling Penny what a wonderful evening it had been, the hour was very late indeed.

"Two o'clock!" Gran exclaimed, yawning widely. "I

can't think when I've stayed up so late—or had so much fun. It was a grand party, Penny."

"Everyone seemed to enjoy it," Penny nodded, slipping her feet out of her pumps and rubbing her insteps ruefully. "I had a wonderful time myself. You were swell to help with everything."

"Lucius and I had a fine time," Gran chuckled. "And now, I'm going to bed. The kitchen's a shambles, but we'll feel more like coping with it tomorrow."

"I'll just put my corsage in the refrigerator," Penny said. "Then I'm going to bed, too."

But alone in the kitchen, she stood for a long dreaming moment, with Mike's flowers cradled in her palm. They were turning a little brown around the edges; their fresh sweetness had grown just a bit cloying now. Or so an unbiased observer might have thought. But not Penny. To her dazzled eyes the corsage Mike had given her was as beautiful as it had been when first she took it from its nest of sheltering tissue. And however wonderful Pam's dance might have been, Penny wouldn't have traded the evening just past with her for anything in the world.

Chapter Fourteen

PENNY LEARNS THE HARD
WAY

$\mathcal{L}$YING late abed the next morning, Pam and Penny discussed their respective New Year's Eves in detail. The dance had been wonderful, according to Pam. She proceeded to tell Penny all about it. There had been only one flaw.

"Honestly," Pam leaned her chin on her palm the better to see Penny in the bed next to hers, "you can't imagine how Paul Gerard hung around Mother. Randy's father danced with her, of course. So did several other friends of the Kirkpatricks. But Paul—well, he couldn't seem to get her away from them fast enough. Penny, I'm worried. He acts as if he's seriously interested. I wish Mother didn't have to spend so much time at Randy's house. I mean, I think it'll only add fuel to the fire."

"If she's doing over their house," Penny objected, "I don't see how she can stay away. Anyway, Pam, it's her own business. I mean, if she and Randy's uncle should fall in love—"

"Don't just lie there and act as if it's inevitable," Pam interrupted. "We certainly have a right to do what we can."

"I don't see why," Penny argued. "Anyway, they're

probably just friends. It may never amount to anything more than that."

"You," Pam informed her, "didn't see them last night, the way they looked into each other's eyes, the way they danced, as if they were enjoying it so thoroughly."

"Mother hasn't had a chance to dance and have fun for a long while," Penny pointed out. "Most likely she'd have enjoyed herself whoever she went with."

"And that gorgeous white orchid corsage he brought her—" Pam broke off suddenly to send a look of inquiry Penny's way. "That reminds me, I noticed you had a corsage in the refrig last night when I put Mother's and mine away. Who from?"

"Mike," Penny admitted, feeling a pleasant warm glow.

"Mike?" Pam repeated in obvious astonishment. Then she asked, "How come he's throwing his money around so freely?"

"I guess he's had a little more to throw around since he works at McKee's," Penny suggested.

"Maybe I should help him spend it." Pam lay back on her pillows and stretched luxuriously.

It was Penny's turn to lean up on one elbow, the better to look at Pam. She asked, "Will you tell me something?"

"I might," Pam said.

"Who do you really like best?" Penny pressed. "Randy or Mike or Joe or—"

"Do I have to like someone best?" Pam broke in smiling. "They're all so nice."

"I thought maybe you had a preference," Penny's tone was a shade wistful. "You go out most often with Randy."

"Have you been keeping records?" Pam teased. Her

eyes narrowed just a little. "Why this sudden concern over my love life? You needn't worry. I can handle it."

Penny had no doubt that she could.

Once the holidays were past, it was only a hop-skip-and-a-jump until the twins' birthday on the twentieth of January. But during those weeks just before she was seventeen, something quite wonderful happened to Penny.

The first time Mike phoned and asked to speak to her, not Pam, Penny could scarcely believe her ears. Then she thought he must be calling about some *Crier* business. But no! It developed that he wanted her to go with him to the Drama Club play the following Friday. He was asking her, Penny, for a date! As soon as she could manage sufficient breath for speaking, Penny said she'd love to go. After their conversation was over, she hung up and drifted into the bedroom, her feet scarcely seeming to touch the floor.

The pale winter sunshine streaming in the window was much brighter than it had been a few minutes before. The checked gingham drapes seemed more vivid. Gran's voice, lustily singing along with the kitchen radio sounded much more melodious than usual. When Pam came in a little later, she found Penny lying face upward across her bed, smiling beatifically at the ceiling.

"For cri-yi!" Pam said in surprise. "What are you so happy about?"

Gradually Penny's shining gaze focused on her twin's face. "Oh," she said, "it's you. I didn't hear you come in."

Pam chuckled. "That I can believe. You were a million miles away. What on earth were you dreaming about?"

Penny said, her smile warm and confident, "I wasn't dreaming. Something nice just happened."

She proceeded to tell Pam about it. When she had finished, Pam's expression had altered from initial astonishment to studied indifference. "That's swell," she said rather flatly.

"Pam, tell me, did Mike ask you first?" Penny had to know. It was vitally important. She braced herself for her sister's answer by reflecting that it was better to be second choice than not to be asked to go out with Mike at all.

But Pam shook her head in the negative. "No, he didn't. Not that I could have gone with him, if he had. Joe Henderson asked me a week ago. We're double-dating with Laurie McGregor and Randy."

"We're double-dating with Maggie and Bob," Penny confided. Happiness was a warm glow within her. She hadn't been second choice, after all.

Penny couldn't have enjoyed the play more if it had been the newest Broadway hit. Sitting next to Mike in the high school auditorium, laughing at and applauding the far-from-professional efforts of the cast, she had a wonderful time. So, apparently, did Mike. Afterwards, with Maggie and Bob, they wedged themselves into the crowded Hangout for malteds. Over in a corner booth, Penny caught a glimpse of Pam in the midst of her supersmooth crowd. But as the twins waved at each other, Penny felt no slightest twinge of envy.

Funny, she thought, how her viewpoint had changed in a few short months. No longer did she feel insecure and self-conscious. And it was surprising how many friends she had made, since she had struck out for herself and stopped drifting along in her sister's wake. Her popularity would never equal Pam's, nor be as effortless. Penny had to work harder to make people notice and like her, but certainly the result was worth the effort. Tonight as she stood with Mike and Maggie and Bob in the crowd around the Hangout fountain, ever so many people stopped to speak to her as they passed by. Maybe they weren't so sophisticated as Pam's friends, but Penny liked them the better for that, she felt more at ease with them. And, feeling Mike's shoulder press against hers, as someone squeezed past him, Penny felt a glow of complete contentment.

After that night was over, Penny was half afraid to count on another date with Mike. He had said he enjoyed himself, that they must do something again soon. Still, she was doubtful. But her doubts proved unfounded. Mike took her out several more times during the weeks that followed. They went ice skating and to the movies. Often, after they had been working on the *Crier*, Mike would suggest stopping at the Hangout on their way home from school for a Coke or a malted.

Penny was so happy it scared her a little. This was better than her dreams, because this was real, this wonderful gradually ripening friendship with Mike. No longer did she have to imagine how it would be to indulge in long discussions with him on every subject under the sun. They talked about books and poetry, school questions, life in general. Mike wanted to get into newspaper work later on, he told Penny quite a bit about his aims and ambitions. And Penny listened, interested, flattered by Mike's confidence. It didn't even seem odd to her that Mike so seldom spoke of Pam. Or, at least, it didn't strike her as odd until later.

Pam, on the other hand, quite often spoke of Mike to Penny. She couldn't, she admitted, see what Penny found so fascinating about him.

"Honestly," she said, "the way you hang on his slightest word is silly! What's so wonderful about Mike Bradley? Randy's much better looking."

"That," Penny said, "is a matter of opinion. I think Mike's better looking."

Pam shrugged. "You shouldn't be so obvious about it though. It's a mistake to let a man realize you think he's so terrific. It goes to his head."

Penny said confidently, "Mike's not like that."

"You needn't talk as though I don't know what Mike's like," Pam's tone carried a note of exasperation. "I've gone out with him, too."

"I know," Penny said. "You probably know him as well, or better, than I do. But we're good friends, Mike and I. And when two people are friends—well, it just seems as if they understand each other."

Pam sighed. An annoyed sigh. Penny thought, "If she didn't have more dates than she can keep up with, I'd almost think she was jealous. But that's silly. . . ."

Later, looking back, it was easy for Penny to see different signposts that should have caught her attention sooner, had she not been so blinded by her admiration for Mike. The way he never spoke of Pam and seemed anxious to hurry on to some other subject when Penny brought her sister's name into the conversation. The way he was particularly attentive to Penny whenever Pam happened to be around. The way he always wanted to go to the Hangout, where Pam was especially likely to see him and Penny together. But Penny, happily blind and blindly happy, didn't notice.

She did notice that Pam went out of her way to be nice to Mike, at school, or whenever they encountered each other accidentally. Pam would turn on the full blast of her charm, smiling up at Mike provocatively, using all the little winning devices at which she was so adept. And Penny's heart would quiver within her and she would hope hard that Mike could hold out against Pam's wiles, that their friendship was stronger than the former attraction Pam had held for him.

And then there came a night when Pam went to the movies with Joe Henderson and Mike dropped over to see Penny. Mother was playing bridge at the Kirkpatricks and Gran went to bed fairly early to read a detective story. When Pam and Joe got home, they found Penny and Mike sprawled comfortably on the floor in front of the record player, a big bowl of popcorn between them, listening raptly to Liszt.

"Honestly!" Pam exclaimed, stepping over them in disdain and sitting down on the couch. "You two long-hairs!"

Joe flopped down comfortably beside her. He grinned at Mike, asking, "You can get away with an evening like this? Pam's more expensive to entertain, I can tell you!"

"Yes," Mike said, "I know."

He was looking directly at Pam as he said it. Pam didn't say anything. She simply sat there, looking at Mike.

"That's right," Joe chuckled. "You switched twins in midstream, didn't you?"

The silly words, the rich sweet music in the background scarcely touched Penny's consciousness. She was aware only of the way Pam and Mike were looking deep into each other's eyes, each unwilling, or unable, to withdraw his gaze. Watching them, it seemed as though a heavy hand closed around Penny's heart. Something in that look passing between Pam and Mike was too revealing. Penny couldn't ignore it, or pretend it wasn't happening, much as she would have liked to. Why, she thought, the old spark of Mike's interest in Pam hadn't died. She had simply persuaded herself that this was the case because she wanted so desperately to believe it. But Mike was just as crazy about Pam as ever. His look revealed that clearly.

Penny told herself, "It should be plain enough, even to a dope like you. You were even the one who told him how to get her interested again. Play hard-to-get, you told him. Don't let her see she's got you where she wants you."

So Mike had followed her advice. He had even gone farther and pretended to be interested in someone else. It had started on New Year's Eve, when he brought this someone else a corsage.

"You fell for it hook, line and sinker," Penny reminded herself. "Every time he asked you for a date, you were only too eager to accept. You believed he really liked you, because that was what you wanted to believe. And because you were friends, it didn't occur to you that Mike would use you as a decoy. But it's really Pam he wants, it's always been Pam."

The bitter hurt within Penny swelled and grew until it seemed that her body wasn't big enough to contain it. She was vaguely aware of voices carrying on some kind of conversation. She even took part in it, to some extent. But she held one of the records she had taken from its album so tightly that it snapped under the pressure.

"Hey!" Mike said, grinning at her. "Don't you know your own strength?"

He picked up the pieces of the record and Penny took them from him and dropped them into the waste basket. "It wasn't a very good one," she said.

And then the voices went on, her own among them. And eventually the hateful evening was over.

Lying in bed in the dark, long after Pam had fallen asleep, Penny kept her arms locked tight across her chest to hold the hurt in. She wouldn't go out with Mike again. She wouldn't continue being merely a means by which he could win Pam back. Let Pam have him if she wanted him. She was welcome.

But hot tears squeezed themselves from under Penny's lashes and she thought despairingly, "Oh, Mike, Mike, how could you treat me this way, when I thought we were friends? How could you hurt me so?"

It wasn't like Mike to be inconsiderate, or cruel. His feeling for Pam must simply have blinded him to the effect of his scheme on Penny. Or maybe he had thought she realized what he was doing from the start.

But she hadn't. She had taken his pretended interest for the real thing. And now, lying there in the sheltering dark, Penny knew that tonight had ended even her friendship with Mike. For there were some things friendship couldn't survive and a lack of honesty was one of them.

Chapter Fifteen

AN APOLOGY

$\mathcal{P}$ENNY took a quick prelim-
inary look into the *Crier* office to satisfy herself that Mike
wasn't alone there. She had been avoiding him except in
the company of others for more than a week now. And
she meant to go right on doing so. But this afternoon Bob
Purcell was draped across a corner of Mike's desk, arguing
some matter with him. And Maggie Wright and another
reporter were diligently searching for something in the
back files. So Penny went on in.

"Hi," she greeted all of them casually. Then, to Bob,
she said, "Here's the report of the Student Council meeting."

"All written up, I hope," Bob said, taking the sheets of
paper she handed him.

Penny nodded. "I'm afraid it's a little late."

"Yeah, Mike's been beefing about it," Bob admitted.

"You're darn right, I was beefing," Mike growled. "That
report should have been in yesterday, Penny, and you
know it!"

"Brother, is he in a mood!" Bob ambled over to a typewriter and inserted a blank sheet noisily. He began to type
in a brisk staccato outburst of sound.

"I've got a right to be!" Mike frowned at Penny. "I
don't know what's got into you lately. You used to be

the most dependable assistant I had. But now it seems I can't ever find you when I need you. You didn't even show up yesterday after school and, boy, was I snowed under!"

"I was busy," Penny said, her voice low.

She was well aware that Mike had been swamped with work the day before. She had looked in after school, but the fact that he was all alone had stopped her at the door. Of course, she had figured that someone else would be turning up to help him.

"Quit riding her," Maggie said good-humoredly. "Just because she started out working herself down to a nubbin for you doesn't mean she's got to keep it up. She finally got smart, that's all."

Penny gave Maggie a grateful grin. "I can help for a while now," she told Mike. "What do you want me to do?"

He proceeded to tell her and she got to work with her usual quiet competence. For the next hour, while people milled distractingly around the little office, Penny kept her mind on the job at hand. She concentrated so closely that she didn't notice how the crowd was thinning out, until suddenly only she and Maggie and Bob and Mike were left. Fortunately Penny was at a good stopping point.

She said, "This is finished now. And I'll really have to get going. It's after four-thirty. You coming, Maggie?"

Bob Purcell objected, "Not yet she can't. She promised to help me finish the humor column."

"Sorry," Maggie told Penny. "I let him twist my arm."

"It doesn't matter—" Penny began, then broke off as Mike got to his feet and yanked the cover over his type-writer.

"I'm through for the day, too," he said, stretching. "You won't mind closing up when you're finished, will you, Bob?"

As Bob agreed, it seemed to Penny that a rather knowing look passed between the two boys, almost as if this had been prearranged. Was Maggie in on it, too, Penny wondered?

But she had no choice except to cross the journalism room and walk down the corridor to her locker, with Mike ambling along beside her. While she got her coat on, he shrugged into his battered leather jacket. Together, almost silently, they went out through the heavy doors and down the long flight of stone steps.

"How about stopping for a malted?" Mike asked as they reached the street.

But Penny said, "I—think I'd better get home. I've got lots of things to do."

Mike nodded. "That's what I thought you'd say." But instead of letting it go at that and heading in the direction of his own home, he fell doggedly into step with Penny. "Okay," he said, "let's have it. What have I done to make you sore?"

Well, this was it, Penny thought. She had hoped that if she avoided Mike as much as possible, if she treated him with cool civility when chance threw them together, he might gradually get the idea that she had seen through his elaborate ruse to win Pam back. She had thought that when he realized this, he might simply let the whole sorry business drop, without any discussion. But apparently this was not to be the case.

When she didn't answer immediately, Mike went on, his tone actually a little aggrieved, "If you're mad, at least

I've got a right to know why. I'm entitled to some explanation."

"*You're* entitled to an explanation!" Penny glared up at him, stopped in her tracks. "Well, I like that! After the way you've treated me, Mike Bradley, using me as—as nothing but a come-on to get Pam interested in you again!"

Mike stood there, looking down at her rather shamedly, thrown a bit off balance by her unaccustomed anger. He said, "But, gee, Penny, I didn't think you'd be sore. I thought you realized all along what I was doing. Why, it was you who put the idea in my head."

Penny's jaw jutted out grimly. "I told you how Pam was, but that didn't mean I was willing to co-operate in your schemes—not if I'd known what you were up to! I don't think it was fair—or—or kind—" she stopped talking before her voice broke up entirely.

"Gee, Penny," there was real regret in Mike's tone, "I didn't realize you'd feel like that."

"Well, I do," Penny said hotly. "When two people are friends, as I thought we were, they shouldn't have to examine each other's motives to be sure one of them isn't taking advantage of the other. You ought to be able to depend on your friends."

"Penny," Mike said, gripping her elbow, "listen to me. I told you I thought you realized what I was doing. You've got to believe that."

There was no doubting the sincerity of his tone, of his blue eyes looking down so steadily into hers. Penny felt the first hot glow of her rage begin to die down a little.

Mike's voice went on, "I should have come right out and asked you if you'd help me. But I honestly thought you understood. After that talk we had that day in the drugstore, when you gave me that steer on Pam—well, I guess I just figured you'd be willing to go a little further and help me get her interested again. I—guess I thought that because I knew we were friends. And I figured the same way you do, that friends can count on each other. Why, Penny, I didn't mean to hurt your feelings, or make you mad. I guess I've just been pretty stupid about the whole thing. But you can't condemn a guy for stupidity, can you?"

Of one accord they started to walk on slowly, Mike still gripping Penny's elbow. After a few steps, she admitted, "I guess I was pretty stupid, too, or I'd have realized sooner what you were trying to do. After all, I—knew how you felt about Pam."

It wasn't fair, she realized, to blame Mike because her own eyes had been so dazzled with dreams she hadn't been able to see clearly. Why would he realize she was letting her imagination run wild, convincing herself that he had got over Pam, just because that was what she so desperately wanted to believe?

"No," Mike argued, "it was my fault. I realize that now. I had a lot of nerve, just taking it for granted that you'd help me get Pam back. I'm sorry, Penny, will you forgive me?"

She nodded. "But count me out of your schemes. If you want to keep on making Pam jealous, you'll have to get yourself another girl."

Mike said, "Maybe that won't be necessary. She's been pretty nice to me lately. But you and I are still friends. Remember that."

"I will," Penny told him, her throat aching.

"Okay," Mike said. "Now is there any reason a couple of friends can't have malteds together at the Hangout?"

"I guess not," Penny said. She even had to laugh a little. . . .

The next time Mike called up, it was Pam he asked for. And Pam, airily disregarding a tentative date with a new man in her life named Peterson, said she'd love to go to the movies and what time would Mike be over?

That settled, she came into the dining alcove where Penny was laying the table for dinner. "What do you know!" Pam exclaimed with a slight lilt in her voice. "That was Mike."

"Was it?" Penny asked, arranging the silverware with geometrical precision.

"He asked me to go to the show with him," Pam said.

"That's nice," Penny said calmly. "It's a cute show. Maggie and I saw it last night."

Pam stared at her for a moment, the slightest hint of a frown wrinkling her brow. "Don't you care?" she asked then: "After all, Mike's been taking you out more often lately than he has me."

"Oh, well," Penny's shoulders in her yellow sweater moved in a little shrug. "He can ask anyone he wants to for a date, I guess." She glanced up from her task to Pam's face then, her gray eyes inquiring. "But I thought you were going to play table tennis with Pete."

"That wasn't definite," Pam said. "He was going to call up first. I'll just tell him something else has come up. Unless," she added, "you'd like to play table tennis with him?"

"In your place?" Penny said drily. "We haven't tried to pull a switch on a boy in a long while, Pam."

"They always used to get onto it when we did," Pam remembered with a little reminiscent smile. "I'll never forget that time in the city when I talked you into going to the movies with my date, because another boy had asked me to go dancing and I thought that sounded like more fun."

Penny wouldn't forget it, either. The anguish she had suffered, trying to be talkative and vivacious like Pam, trying to keep the boy—his name had been Harry something—fooled into thinking she was Pam. But it hadn't worked. He had been pretty angry with them both for a while over the attempted deception. But Pam had got around him, as she always managed to get around boys. It had been Penny he held a grudge against.

Pam said thoughtfully, "I'm not so sure you couldn't get away with pretending to be me now. You've got a lot more poise than you used to have. Of course, you don't talk as much as I do, but I doubt Pete knows us well enough to tell the difference."

Penny said, "Don't be silly. I haven't any intention of going out on your date with Pete. You just get yourself out of it the best you can."

"Okay," Pam said. "It was just an idea."

She went on into the bedroom, humming happily under her breath. Penny's lips twisted into a wry smile. A date with Mike wouldn't have pleased Pam nearly this much a month ago. Apparently his well-laid plan was working.

Later that evening, after Pam had gone out with Mike, Paul Gerard called up and invited himself over for a bridge game. Lucius Hancock was always available for a fourth, so he and Gran and Mother and Paul were sitting around the card table in the living room, when the doorbell rang and Penny went downstairs to answer it. Rather to her surprise, she saw Randy Kirkpatrick standing on the doorstep.

"Why—hello," she said. "Pam wasn't expecting you, was she?"

Randy shook his head. "I suppose she isn't home."

"No, she's not," Penny admitted.

Randy sighed. "Oh, well, I guess that was too much to hope for. Anyway," he went on, "I'm starving. How about you coming out to the Lighthouse with me for a hamburger?"

"Why—okay," Penny said, even more surprised than before.

Randy followed her upstairs and kibitzed at the bridge table while Penny got her coat. Then they went out together into the chill clear winter night. Penny hadn't ridden in the green convertible for quite a long while. Randy switched on the radio and music spilled out sweetly.

He asked, his tone rather glum, "Who'd Pam go out with?"

Penny told him and apparently it wasn't the answer he expected. He said, "I thought Mike had been concentrating on you lately."

"Oh, I wouldn't say concentrating," Penny murmured as lightly as she could. "We've just dated a few times."

Randy brooded for a while in silence. Then he said, "I guess once you get a yen for Pam, you don't get over it easily."

"I guess not," Penny agreed.

The Lighthouse was warm and brightly lighted, well-filled with customers for a week night, and gay with juke-box music. The hamburgers and French fries were delicious. Randy's conversation did seem to keep veering around to Pam, but Penny didn't mind listening to his troubles. She ate and put in a sympathetic word now and then, which seemed to be all Randy expected of her. At least, Penny was glad to see that his appetite wasn't impaired. He ate three hamburgers, a piece of apple pie à la mode and drank a malted, while all Penny could hold was one hamburger and a chocolate soda.

Once Randy asked anxiously, "Will you tell me the truth about something, Penny?"

"Of course."

"Do you think Pam likes me as well as any of the rest of the guys who are always hanging around her?"

Penny nodded emphatically. But that was as far as she meant to commit herself. The last time she had had a conversation like this, it had been with Mike Bradley. And she had made the mistake of going on to suggest to Mike how he could get Pam more interested in him. She wasn't going to stick her neck out again. She wasn't going to say another word on the subject. Let Randy and Mike and all of them figure Pam out for themselves.

The next time there was a lull in Randy's tale of woe, Penny merely intended to point out that it was time they were getting home. That was the safest way. . . .

Chapter Sixteen

DISAPPOINTMENT

ONE night early in February, Penny asked Pam bluntly, "Who are you going to invite to the Cupid Caper?"

This was the valentine dance, sponsored by the Girls' Athletic Club, where the customary dating procedure was reversed and the girls asked the boys to be their guests for the evening.

Pam, creaming her face at the dressing table preparatory to going to bed, glanced around curiously. "I haven't quite decided," she said. "Why? Did you want to ask Mike?"

"Well," Penny said slowly, "not exactly. I was thinking of asking Randy, if you didn't have him in mind."

"Randy?" Pam's brows lifted in astonishment. "Since when have you two been on such chummy terms?"

"Oh, it isn't that," Penny denied. "But I felt sort of sorry for him the other night when he dropped over and you were out with Mike. I think Randy's getting the idea he's being lost in the shuffle." She brushed her hair a couple of strokes before adding thoughtfully, "So, I figured if you weren't going to ask him to the Caper, maybe I would. I thought we might double-date."

Pam said drily, "You're getting to be such a sympathetic listener lately everyone's telling you his troubles."

Penny grinned at her and, after an unwilling moment,

Pam grinned back. Penny asked, "Can I help it if you've got so many guys on the string, you can't keep them all happy?"

Pam chuckled. "I guess I have been letting Randy down a little. But to tell you the truth, I was seriously thinking of asking him to the Caper. I'm really quite fond of Randy," she admitted.

"Are you?" Penny asked.

Pam nodded. "I like Mike a lot, too, though," she said thoughtfully. "I guess when you get right down to it, those two are tops with me."

Penny had suspected that for a long time. The rest of Pam's boy friends came and went and shifted. Randy and Mike seemed practically permanent.

Pam turned all the way around from the mirror to look straight at Penny. "I will ask Randy," she decided. "So if you'd like to ask Mike, go right ahead. And let's double-date like you said. It would be fun."

"Well," Penny said consideringly, "I'll think about asking Mike. But don't rush me. . . ."

She was inwardly a little surprised at the way things had turned out. It always surprised her when the rudimentary principles of psychology worked so smoothly. She had been quite sincere in telling Pam she was thinking of asking Randy to the dance. But that statement of hers seemed to have tipped the scales of Pam's favor toward Randy, too. Penny wondered, "If I'd thought about asking Mike in the first place, I wonder if Pam would have decided he was the one she wanted?" But there was no sense in going into that, even mentally. All she need do now was to screw up her courage and ask Mike to go to the Caper with her.

As a matter of fact, Mike himself brought up the subject the next time he and Penny happened to be alone together.

Penny was checking over the Personals and Mike had just finished proof-reading an editorial when he asked, out of a clear sky, "You know something? I just thought of a keen way you can prove you really have forgiven me for the stinking way I treated you a while back."

"How's that?" Penny asked, glancing up.

"Invite me to the Caper," Mike said.

Penny's heart beat a bit faster. But she said lightly, "Oh, I could, could I?"

"Sure," Mike said, grinning. "Unless you've already asked someone else."

"No," Penny admitted. "I haven't yet."

"Okay, then," Mike went on coaxingly. "I'll think you're still mad at me unless you do."

Penny said, smiling a little, "Well, I'm not mad, so I guess I'll have to ask you if that's how you feel about it."

"Fine," Mike beamed. "I accept."

"Shall we double-date with Pam and Randy?" Penny asked.

"I don't care," Mike said. "Whatever you'd like."

And so it was decided that the four of them would go together. It all seemed so simple and effortless, after all her preliminary fretting and fuming over the matter. That was always the way, Penny thought wryly. The things you worried about never worked out as you expected them to. She was to learn that it was the things you didn't worry about that threw you.

The next couple of weeks whirled past in a pleasant dream for Penny. Gran made her a new formal, as she had promised. It was pale green taffeta with a stiff little peplum of black lace, very becoming to Penny's height and slimness. Pam felt a little abused over having to wear a dress from last year, but Mother was adamant, despite the fact that business at Howard House was good and her commission on the almost completed Kirkpatrick job a substantial one.

She told Pam, "If I start getting you new formals for every dance, I'll go broke in no time. You've only worn your yellow one once."

Pam said, "It wouldn't do for this dance. I wore it New Year's Eve and I was out with Randy then, too."

The amused glint in Mother's eye indicated that she did not consider this argument absolutely unanswerable. But Pam went on before she could say anything, "Never mind. I'll wear my ice blue from the Prom last year. Randy's never seen that one."

The Cupid Caper was to be held on the Saturday night before Valentine's Day. All that week, Penny could scarcely contain her excitement. The weather was typical of February, slush and icy rain. But the dismal gray of the sky could have been bright sunny blue for all the effect it had on Penny's soaring spirits. The more she thought about Mike actually asking her to invite him to the dance, the more wonderful it seemed. And it wasn't, she had learned by questioning Pam, because he had found out first that Pam was going with someone else. Of course, Penny reminded herself, it could have been his conscience needling him. Maybe he still felt guilty over the way he had taken advantage of her friendship. But, on the other hand, maybe he really preferred to go to the Caper with her.

Penny swung back and forth giddily between doubt and delight.

The last few days before the dance crawled like so many turtles. By Friday afternoon, Penny actually felt sick and headachey with anticipation. At least, she thought it was anticipation until she began to sniff and sneeze around dinner time. Even Gran's good dinner tasted flat and unsavory.

Penny murmured, getting up just before dessert was brought in, "I don't think I want any. I'm going to lie down."

Mother gave her a troubled, sympathetic look. "I do hope you're not getting a bad cold."

"Of course, she isn't," Pam said staunchly, her eyes on Penny's face. "There are so many colds at school, it's hard to keep from picking up a teensy germ."

"It won't amount to anything," Penny said.

But crawling into bed and pressing her hot cheek into the pillow, Penny wondered whom she was trying to convince, Mother or herself?

Mother brought her in a fizzling drink a little later and took her temperature. "Oh, dear," she said, frowning down at the thermometer, "I was afraid you had one."

"I'll be okay," Penny said thickly, as Mother tucked her in.

But she felt worse by morning, alternately hot and cold. Her throat was scratchy, her eyes inclined to water. Pam, her face grave with sympathy, brought her breakfast on a tray. But all Penny wanted was fruit juice.

"If this isn't the foulest development," Pam said unhappily. "Mother's called the doctor."

"Oh, no!" Penny moaned. It wasn't that she didn't like

cheerful, well-groomed Dr. Everett. But to have a doctor made her illness such a positive thing—and she just couldn't be ill! Not really! Not today of all days!

Mother and Gran and Pam hovered around her sympathetically till the doctor came. Flu, that was what Penny had. Bed till further notice, Dr. Everett prescribed firmly. Two kinds of medicine.

"But I'm going to a dance tonight," Penny insisted.

The doctor was sorry, but she'd better have someone get in touch with her young man and break the sad news to him. She was not going to any dance. Penny managed not to cry until after the doctor had gone. But it was a good thing he left quickly, because she couldn't have held out very long. Miserably Penny buried her head under the covers.

Everyone came to the bedroom door to commiserate with her. The muffled blur of Pam's and Gran's and Mother's voices penetrated but vaguely to Penny. It was a shame, they all agreed. They were terribly, terribly sorry.

Penny sniffed almost inaudibly, "Will you call Mike, Pam?" She didn't take her head out from under the covers.

She heard Pam's regretful voice saying, "Yes, I will, Penny. But it's just awful!"

After a while Penny fell into a fitful sleep.

She slept the greater part of the time for the next couple of days, waking to eat when food was pressed upon her, to take her medicine. Once she noticed a little cluster of pink rosebuds in a white vase on her bedside table.

"Those are from Mike," Mother, who was bringing her a tall eggnog explained. "Your corsage for the dance—and he said to tell you he was awfully sorry you're ill."

Penny nodded miserably. "It would have to happen right at this time."

Mother patted her shoulder gently. "That's the way things go sometimes. But there'll be other dances."

Pam was sleeping in Mother's room these nights, but she hovered often in the doorway to talk to Penny. By Monday evening Penny was feeling enough better to be curious about several things. The dance, for one.

"Was it nice?" she asked Pam wistfully.

Pam nodded, her gray eyes suspiciously bright. "Yes, it was. Gee, I wish you could have been there! The decorations were super—big white spider webs all around, with hearts in them instead of spiders. And ever so many people asked about you and were sorry to hear you were sick. I didn't realize how many friends you have, honestly!"

Penny felt a warm little glow of pleasure. Pam wouldn't make up a thing like that just so she'd feel good. It must be true.

"What did Mike say when you called up and told him I couldn't go?" she asked then.

"Well, he felt terribly about it, of course. He was disappointed and all—who wouldn't be? But he seemed to feel worse about your having the flu than about missing the dance."

"Did he really?" Penny asked.

Pam nodded emphatically. "He sent your corsage anyway. But he wouldn't go to the Caper stag, as he could have. And he's called up every single day to see how you're doing."

Penny sighed, a small sigh of sheer pleasure.

"You know something?" Pam said. "I'm beginning to think you're the one Mike likes best around here, not me."

It seemed to Penny that there was note of regret in her sister's tone. She said, "Oh, Mike and I are friends, that's all. You're the one he's really got a yen for."

"I'm not so sure of that any more," Pam said. "Not so sure at all."

Penny asked then, "Did you and Randy have fun at the dance? Tell me all about it."

Pam proceeded to do so. But as Penny listened, her thoughts strayed a little from Pam's enthusiastic recounting of all the fun and excitement of the Cupid Caper. Was there, she wondered wistfully, even the ghost of a chance that Pam was right about Mike liking her best? Pam probably didn't even mean it, Penny told herself firmly. Most likely it was just a kind sisterly ruse to make her convalescence a little happier. If so, it was very sweet of Pam, because the ruse was certainly serving its purpose. Right then, in spite of everything, Penny felt wonderful.

Chapter Seventeen

PENNY HAS AN IDEA

"*F*ine thing!" Mike said on Penny's first day back at school after her bout of flu. "The lengths some people will go to break a date! You could have come right out and told me you'd changed your mind, you know."

Penny kidded back, "I know, but that might have hurt your feelings."

"Yeah," Mike nodded. "I bruise easily." He said then, his blue eyes steady on hers, "It was a darn' shame, that's what it was."

"I know," Penny said, her voice a little husky. She grinned up at him, "Got any work for me around here?"

They were standing in the cluttered *Crier* office and Mike answered, "There's always work around here. Want to write up some club news for me? I've got an editorial to dope out."

"Sure," Penny said.

She gathered up the scribbled club meeting notes that someone had written, while Mike went over and sat down at his typewriter. Maggie Wright came in and got busy, after greeting Penny joyfully. It all seemed nice and usual and Penny was glad to be back. People came and went. Mrs. Gebhard, the journalism teacher came in for a brief conference with Mike. In between interruptions, Mike

pecked away at the typewriter, but it seemed to Penny
that he was throwing away more sheets than he was keeping. Every now and then he would crouch for a while
like Rodin's Thinker, chewing his knuckles thoughtfully.

"Having troubles?" Penny asked, when she laid the finished club news on his desk.

"Sure am," Mike admitted. "Say, Penny," he said then,
"it's March and that's practically spring. Maybe I'll do
that editorial we were talking about a while back."

"About the Prom?" Penny remembered.

"Yeah," Mike said, "and how a lot of the senior girls
work on it, but don't get to go."

"It's a crime!" Maggie spoke vehemently. "We're all
getting fed up! Half the guys ask juniors or sophomores
and the seniors get left out in the cold."

"Unless they've got a regular man of their own," Beth
Conover, a tall blond girl who had just come in, added
emphatically. "It's not fair at all!"

"Now wait a minute," Mike said. "I'm outnumbered.
Hey, Bob," he called to Bob Purcell, who had gone out
into the journalism room on some errand or other, "come
back here and lend me moral support. I've got a lot of
huffy females to deal with."

The ensuing argument waxed hot and long, Bob and
Mike upholding the male prerogative to ask whomever
they wanted to the Prom, Penny and Maggie and Beth
standing firm on their contention that the senior girls
weren't getting a square deal.

"But they can ask juniors if they want to," Bob insisted.
"They can ask guys who've already graduated, anyone
they like."

"Some of them do that," Penny agreed. "Ask older

fellows, that is. But not all of us have an older man on the string to invite. As for asking juniors, if we did that deliberately we'd be razzed to death and you know it."

"Then there isn't any solution of the problem," Mike shrugged. "So what's the use doing an editorial about it and getting everybody all het up?"

"Maybe," Penny said thoughtfully, "there is a solution."

"What?" four voices asked simultaneously.

"I was reading something the other day in a magazine," Penny said. "It told about a date bureau that had been set up in some college, so that students who didn't know a lot of people, or didn't know them well enough to ask for dates, could register there. Then whoever had charge of it matched the registration cards up according to interests, types and all. That way a lot of people got acquainted and went out together who might never have met otherwise."

"I didn't know college students were that shy," Bob said drily.

But Penny said, "Some of them must be. This article gave the name of the college and everything. And it said the idea worked out fine and was very popular with the students."

"Now wait a minute," Mike said. "Let me get this straight. Are you suggesting we set up a date bureau like that here at Glen High?"

"Just for the Prom," Penny told him. It seemed as if the idea were growing and taking more solid shape in her mind as she outlined it. "We could call it Prom Dates, or something like that. And the *Crier* could sponsor it, give it some good publicity. It would work this way. If a girl wanted to go to the Prom and didn't figure she had much chance of being asked, she could register with the bureau. Just senior girls, of course, because after all, it's the senior Prom. But in addition to dateless senior boys, we'd let junior boys who were willing to date senior girls register, too. That way, there ought to be enough to go around and if the bureau matched them up, the girls wouldn't feel funny about going with younger boys. Or at least I shouldn't think they would." Her questioning glance went to Maggie, to Beth.

"It sounds super to me," Beth said.

And Maggie nodded vigorously. "I think so, too."

"It could be a Dutch treat deal," Beth suggested. "That way a lot of guys without too much cash wouldn't be scared to register. Still, they wouldn't feel queer about it, as they would if they actually asked a girl to go fifty-fifty on expenses."

Mike's and Bob's glances met thoughtfully as the girls chattered enthusiastically on. "What do you think?" Mike asked.

Bob wagged his head ruefully. "I hate to say so in front of her, but I think the girl's just had a terrific idea."

"It sounds okay to me, too," Mike had to admit.

"Why, man," Bob exclaimed, "it'll tap that big untouched reservoir of fellas who haven't quite got the nerve or the cash to ask a girl to the Prom! And if you don't think the girls'll go for it, listen to these three yackety-yacketting over it before Penny's idea has hardly had time to take shape."

"Yeah," Mike said wonderingly, "listen . . ."

Two weeks later, with full faculty approval, the *Crier* ran an editorial entitled, "Why Should Any Senior Girl Be A Forgotten Woman at Prom-time?" In writing it,

Mike had waxed eloquent on the subject. "Only senior students and their guests may attend the Prom," he had written. "But every senior man who asks a junior or sophomore or even (pardon the expression!) a freshman girl to the dance, does one of his own contemporaries out of a possible date by so doing. Unfair as this practice obviously is, we have little hope of changing it. However, Penny Howard, one of the reporters on this paper, has come up with a scheme to give the senior girls a break." Mike then proceeded to outline the basic idea of the Prom Dates bureau in detail. Interested students, his editorial explained, would fill out a simple application blank with such information as name, age, height, weight and general type of date wanted. This registration would be open only to senior girls who weren't averse to paying their own way, and to junior and senior men who were willing to escort a senior to the Prom. The committee in charge of the project would then attempt to match up prospective dates on the basis of the information supplied on the registration cards. A booth would be set up for such registration in the hall just outside the journalism room.

The *Crier* came out on Wednesday and, although the Prom was still almost two months off, the "Prom Dates" booth did a flourishing business all that day after school. Penny, who with Beth Conover, had charge of the first day's registrations, was congratulated so many times for her brilliant idea that she felt a warm rosy glow envelop her.

"How does it feel," Beth kidded her good-humoredly, "to be a benefactor of humanity?"

"Wonderful," Penny admitted. "Just wonderful!" She

asked then, "How many names would you say we've got already?"

"Lots," Beth admitted. "Fifty or more, I'll bet. Girls *and* boys," she said enthusiastically. "I was a smidgin scared for fear we'd be swamped with females. But almost as many boys signed up as girls—and this is only the beginning. . . ."

That night at dinner, Pam said, "I think it's really a keen idea, Penny. How did you happen to think of it?"

Penny explained. Mother and Gran seemed as interested as Pam. Penny finished, her cheeks a little flushed, "I didn't know Mike was actually going to put my name in his editorial."

"Why not?" Pam asked. "Credit where credit is due. After all, you thought up the whole thing."

"Yes, but we all talked it over and lots of people made good suggestions. The whole *Crier* staff deserves credit, not just me."

"Don't be modest," Pam admonished. "Let Mike give you a build-up if he wants to. After all the work you've done for him, you've got one coming."

"It was work you liked doing, wasn't it, dear?" Mother said understandingly.

Penny nodded. "I love it. Working on the paper's lots of fun."

"I saw the line-up at your booth after school," Pam said. "It looks as if the idea's catching on in a big way."

"I guess it is," Penny agreed.

It was nice of Pam not to be even a shade supercilious about the whole thing. Girls as popular as she and her friends didn't need anything of the sort, of course. But there were so many others who did. Maybe, Penny thought, she'd be signing up herself one of these days. But not yet. Not quite yet. The Prom wouldn't be held until May. And, as Gran frequently quoted, "Hope springs eternal in the human breast."

Chapter Eighteen

PAM HAS A PROBLEM

$\mathcal{A}$S WINTER warmed and melted into early spring, Howard House hummed with activity. Although Celia had finished her job for the Kirkpatricks, other good commissions followed in its wake, sparked by Ellen Kirkpatrick's enthusiastic satisfaction. The shop was left more and more in Dorothea Crane's capable care, while Celia was occupied with outside work.

Gran, who was always busy, became more so than ever in April. Lucius Hancock fell on the newly waxed floor of his real estate office and broke his leg. So in addition to taking care of the housework and the twins' needs, Gran made frequent trips to cheer up Lucius, whose old bones knit slowly.

"Honestly," Gran said, "it's no wonder poor Lucius gets grumpy. The cast's bad enough. But living all alone, with only that pottering Mrs. Enright to do for him by the day —well, it's very boring for him. And her cooking!" Gran shook her head eloquently. "You should have seen how he enjoyed that angel-food cake I took him."

Another time, Gran might make him a custard, or a rich chicken broth to keep up his strength. Hardly a day passed that she didn't find a moment to stop by and play a game of cribbage with him. But she seemed to thrive on the extra work Lucius made her. Her brisk energy seemed boundless.

Mother continued to see a good deal of Paul Gerard, who was lingering at the Kirkpatricks' long enough to fin- ish a book he was writing. But Penny thought their friend- ship was a fine thing, so much pleasure did both of them seem to derive from it. And Pam had grown more philo- sophical about the whole matter, coming around gradually to Penny's viewpoint that it was, after all, Mother's affair and not theirs.

"It might be fun to have a stepfather," Pam said dream- ily on one occasion, "especially such an attractive one as Paul. And if his book should turn out to be a best-seller, he'll be a celebrity."

"Now you're getting carried away," Penny chuckled. But she was glad Pam had stopped fretting about it. Much as she herself hated the thought of any change in their way of living, Mother's happiness was the important thing.

Then, one evening at dinner, Mother announced quite calmly that Paul would be leaving Glenhurst in a few days.

"Leaving?" Pam exclaimed in surprise.

Penny and Gran looked inquiringly at Mother, too.

"Why, yes," she said. "Is that so astonishing?"

"What about his book?" Penny asked.

"That's finished," Celia said. "He's already sent it off to the publishers. Now he's going to Europe to do a series of articles for a news magazine."

Penny's glance sought Pam's, but Pam was staring won- deringly at Mother. "You mean," she asked, "you don't mind?"

"Mind?" Mother repeated. "Why, it's a wonderful

break for him, dear. A series of key articles in a magazine with a circulation of—"

"I don't mean that," Pam interrupted. "I mean—well, don't you mind personally?"

Mother smiled at her. "I'll miss him, if that's what you're getting at. We're good friends, we've had fun together. I'll certainly look forward to seeing him again, if he ever comes back to visit Ellen."

"But you're not in love with him?" Pam asked.

Mother's smile widened. "Now where did you ever get such a romantic notion as that?" Her amused glance went on to Penny. "Did you think Paul and I were in love, too?"

Gran chuckled drily. "It's their age, Celia. At seventeen girls do a lot of thinking about love. Don't you remember?"

Mother nodded. "I should have remembered. But, darlings, I had no idea you were worried about me."

"We weren't worried, exactly," Penny put in. "At least, I wasn't. I figured if you were in love, it was your own affair."

Mother said, "I'm glad you figured I was old enough not to lose my head." The corners of her mouth tipped up a little.

Pam said indignantly, "Well, I didn't think you'd do that, Mother. But Paul Gerard's a very attractive man. And I was afraid, if you married him, he'd want you to go away—"

"It was just," Penny backed Pam up earnestly, "that we didn't want anything to change. It's so nice living here in Glenhurst, having Howard House and getting to see a lot of you."

"I like it, too," Mother assured them. "And while I won't deny that Paul has a lot of charm, I wouldn't dream of marrying him, even if he wanted to marry me, which he doesn't. In fact, I doubt very much that Paul ever marries. He's too confirmed a bachelor, not at all domestic. And the rootless, wandering sort of life he's lived has too strong a hold on him to be easily broken."

" 'A rolling stone gathers no moss,' " Gran quoted sagely.

Pam asked wonderingly, "And you don't care even a little speck about him going away?"

Penny's eyes, too, were fixed inquiringly on Mother's face. The smile that had been tugging at Mother's mouth won out completely. "Well, I can't honestly say that," she admitted. "At my age, an occasional corsage, and invitation to go dancing, is quite flattering. And Paul plays a good game of bridge. But my heart isn't broken, I assure you. And I'm quite satisfied with my life just as it is."

So that was that.

As spring came on Penny found herself busier than ever, almost as busy as Pam, whose whirl of activity she no longer had any cause to envy. Between school work and dates and their various club activities, neither girl had much time to spare. Pam had more dates than Penny, but Penny was invited out often enough, to the movies, or a basketball game or some other school affair, so that her evenings weren't discouragingly empty. Pam's train of admirers shifted and changed, except for the ever-faithful Randy. Mike, for some reason neither Pam nor Penny wholly understood, had stopped pursuing Pam entirely. Secretly, Penny suspected this was a further result of her advice to him to play disinterested and thus win Pam's favor. But he seemed to be overdoing it a little, in view of Pam's already aroused interest. Penny continued to see a good deal of Mike at school, through their work on the *Crier* and the increasingly active Prom Dates bureau. Often Mike would buy her a Coke at the Hangout on their way home. The easy friendship between them remained the same and Penny enjoyed every aspect of it. But Mike never phoned Pam any more to ask for a date, never dropped over to see her unannounced, as he used to do so often.

"I don't know what's got into the big dope," Pam said indignantly one night as she and Penny were getting ready for bed. "He doesn't act mad or anything, when we happen to run into each other, but—" her voice trailed off unhappily.

Penny said, "Maybe he just got tired of being one of a mob scene."

"But that's silly," Pam argued. "Competition shouldn't discourage a man. According to psychology, it should encourage him, make him want to follow the crowd."

Penny shrugged. "Maybe Mike never studied psychology."

Pam shook her head. "I know he used to be sort of crazy about me. He made it plain enough. But lately— well, I just don't like his attitude. I don't like it at all!"

Penny went into the bathroom to brush her teeth. Pam's voice followed her. "I didn't do a thing to him, either. I didn't break a date or anything. How does he get that way?"

Penny thought of all the boys who hadn't done a thing to Pam, and yet had been given the air when someone new came along. Probably they couldn't understand it, either. Maybe they had felt as Pam was feeling now.

Of course, it wasn't that way with Mike, though, Penny remembered. Mike was still interested in Pam. He must be simply putting on an act. Otherwise Penny couldn't understand his change of attitude any more than Pam could. It just wouldn't make sense.

She squeezed toothpaste onto her brush thoughtfully, as Pam's indignant voice went on and on. When Penny came out of the bathroom, Pam was still talking.

She said decisively, "No man has ever given me a brush-off before! And Mike needn't think he's going to get away with it. I'll show him I'm the one who'll decide when we're through."

Penny inquired, "What are you going to do about it?"

"I'll play up to him," Pam said, "as I've never had to play up to a boy before. Mike has no idea how sweet I'm going to be to him from now on."

"But why?" Penny asked, her voice a little husky from pushing itself around the lump in her throat. "Why do you bother unless you like Mike better than Randy and all the rest?"

"It's a matter of pride now," Pam said, her eyes narrowed determinedly.

Penny made a final effort. "I should think it would be an awful lot of trouble to go to unless you really want him back."

"Maybe I do," Pam admitted. "I've certainly missed him."

Penny sighed, but it was such a small unobtrusive sigh Pam didn't even notice it.

That night Penny dreamed that she and Pam had a bitter quarrel, during which she cried out, "You can't have Mike back—I want him! If you'd just leave him alone, maybe he'd like me. I won't let you start working on him again. I won't!"

In her dream, Pam laughed at her outburst, a harsh, cold laugh, utterly unlike her. Penny woke with that taunting laughter ringing in her ears. But the bedroom was cool and dark and quiet, with only the sound of Pam's even breathing in the bed next to hers.

Penny burrowed her cheek deeper into the pillow and tried to fall asleep again. But her thoughts milled in futile circles. Maybe, if she told Pam how well she liked Mike, it would make a difference. Maybe then Pam would leave him alone. But Penny had too much pride to throw herself on her sister's pity. And Mike, she remembered miserably, didn't want to be left alone. He was trying to get Pam back. That was the basis of his pretended indifference. And now Pam was going to try to get him back. Neither of them, Penny thought bleakly, should have to try very hard.

Her last waking thought was a wry one. She guessed she might as well sign up for Prom Dates after all. . . .

Chapter Nineteen

EVERYTHING HAPPENS AT ONCE

"*H*EY, wait for me," Mike Bradley's voice stopped Penny in her tracks at the top of the school steps.

As he caught up with her a second later, she asked, "Did you take me for Pam?"

But Mike denied this, a little pointed edge to his tone. "I can tell you from Pam all right, even if I haven't seen much of you lately."

They moved on down the long stone flight of steps side by side, a tall girl in a gray wool suit with a tangerine scarf at the throat, a taller boy in brown cords and a tan jacket.

What Mike said was true enough. Penny had been avoiding him since the night when Pam had announced her intentions so frankly. It seemed that every time she saw him around school, Pam was right there beside him, laughing beguilingly up into his face, using all her wiles on him. No wonder Penny had hurried on about her own business, since the sight of Pam and Mike together wasn't exactly pleasant to her.

"What gives?" Mike demanded bluntly. "Am I poison, or something?"

"Of course not," Penny told him. "I've—been pretty busy, working on Prom Dates and all."

"Yeah, I know," Mike said. "We're all busy, with graduation coming up. But could you spare me—" he consulted his wristwatch with mock gravity, "maybe fifteen minutes of your valuable time?"

"Of course," Penny said, amused at his exaggeratedly businesslike manner. "If I forgot something I was supposed to do for the *Crier*—"

She broke off as Mike shook his head. "You didn't forget anything. This is a personal matter. Look," he laid a detaining hand on her arm, "could we stop in the park a little while? There's something I want to ask you."

It would be something concerning Pam, Penny felt sure. Every instinct within her strained against listening to Mike's confidences. But she couldn't very well refuse, so she let him take her where he wished. This turned out to be a bench near the little lake, with birds singing in the tall old trees overhead and a gray squirrel, fat and saucy, frisking close to their feet.

Penny saw no point in dodging the issue. She said, "It looks as if you're all set with Pam again, just as you wanted."

Mike's blue gaze was disconcertingly direct on hers. The soft spring breeze ruffled his hair forward and he shoved it back with an impatient hand. "Who said anything about Pam?"

"Why—no one," Penny admitted in surprise. "But weren't you going to tell me how well your scheme had worked?"

"What scheme?" Mike frowned. "You mean 'way back last winter when I tried to rush you and make her jealous?"

"No," Penny said, "I mean just lately, the way you ignored her for a while. That's what won her over, Mike. Why, her whole attitude toward you has changed."

"You're telling me?" Mike grinned wryly. "But I still don't see why we're discussing Pam. It's us I want to talk about. You," he touched the top button of her jacket, "and me."

"But—" Penny's eyes were so wide with astonishment, the lids felt stretched, "I don't understand."

"For a bright girl," Mike sounded a little uncomfortable, "you're not very bright, if you know what I mean. I think you've got a sister complex. Stop thinking about Pam for a minute and concentrate on you." He leaned a little nearer and Penny was acutely aware of his arm, stretched along the back of the bench behind her, not touching her, but close.

He went on, "It's time you and I got a few things straightened out." He stopped then and was silent for so long, Penny was just about to ask, "What things, Mike?" when he started speaking again in a tone slightly jerky with embarrassment. "A guy hates to come right out and admit he's been a big dope, but that's exactly what I have been."

"A—dope?" Penny repeated blankly.

"D-o-p-e," Mike spelled it out. "You know of a better way to describe a guy who takes months to figure out which girl he likes best? I've been batting my brains for weeks, looking for a reasonable way to explain it to you. The thing is, Penny—" he groped for words, "well, I was dazzled by Pam. That was all it ever amounted to, but I was so dazzled, I managed to convince myself there was more to it than that."

Penny shut her eyes for a minute, trying to get her bearings, trying to believe she was really hearing what she seemed to be hearing. But when Mike went on talking, she opened them again and fixed her rapt, attentive gaze on his face.

Mike admitted, "I think maybe I got the two of you kind of confused in my mind, as if you were one person with two personalities. Sometimes, when I had a date with Pam, it seemed as if something were lacking. The times I enjoyed most were when we just stayed home and you'd be around all evening, too. Am I making any sense at all, Penny?"

She nodded, not quite able to speak. And Mike went on, haltingly, trying to put into words how the magic Pam held for him had dimmed, how he had finally realized that Penny's friendship was more important than anything between Pam and him.

"I should have known sooner," Mike apologized. "The way we always like to talk and kick ideas around, nights like the one when we got to playing records and had such a swell time."

"The sleigh ride," Penny remembered, her mouth curving.

"Yeah," Mike said, "you'd think I'd have seen the light. But, no. Thick-headed, that's me."

"You're not," Penny denied. "You're not a bit."

Pam had always dazzled people, she always would. Penny was glad, though, that Mike had got un-dazzled at last.

"For weeks," Mike told her, "I've been trying to let you know I'd come to my senses. I felt—kind of self-conscious about asking you for a real date after taking you for granted so long. But I didn't date Pam. And I don't intend to."

Mike's indifference, Penny realized, had affected Pam exactly as she had suspected such treatment would. Only she had been mistaken, wonderfully mistaken, Penny saw now, in thinking it was merely pretended indifference. It was the real thing. Mike hadn't been fooling.

The happiness this knowledge brought must have shown through in her face. Because Mike's tone dipped a husky note lower as he said, "Penny, if you don't stop looking at me like that, I'll—"

She felt his hand on her shoulder, pulling her close into the circle of his arm. She knew then for sure that she wasn't dreaming, that Mike was actually saying these wonderful, these incredible things to her. His other hand closed over hers and Penny's fingers felt perfectly at home curled up there.

Mike asked earnestly, "Do you suppose it'll convince Pam if I invite you to the Prom? Because that's what I'm going to do. Will you go with me, Penny?"

She nodded. "I'd love to, Mike." Suddenly though, she remembered something and exclaimed, "Golly, I'll have to get my name out of the Prom Dates file!"

"Relax," Mike chuckled. "I took it out. Just happened to notice it and figured I wanted a chance to ask you first. Gee, Penny," his hand tightened on hers, "you're swell not to hold it against me for being such a dope."

Penny admitted, "I've been pretty dopey, too. When Pam told me she was going to try to get you back—well, I didn't say a word to stop her. I thought it was what you wanted."

Mike shook his head. "How wrong can you get?"

They sat for a time quietly, not needing words to express the new warm understanding between them. Penny thought it wasn't really so strange that Mike had taken a long while to realize that their friendship was more than it seemed. She hadn't realized it herself, she had been afraid to hope too much. She had been firmly convinced that anyone Pam wanted, Pam could get. She suspected that Pam thought that, too. She was in for a rude surprise. How would she take it, Penny wondered? But she was so happy that even the threat of Pam's displeasure couldn't spoil it.

"Oh," Mike spoke suddenly, "there was something else I was going to tell you. Headlines Club has put your name up for Prom Queen."

"My name?" Penny gasped incredulously.

Each club had the privilege of nominating a candidate for the coveted honor. All seniors were eligible to vote and the outcome was a question of popularity. Besides the queen, her court of six attendants was decided upon by the voting. All the most popular girls in the class were among the nominees, including Pam.

"Don't sound so flabbergasted," Mike teased. "You're pretty darn' popular, especially since you dreamed up the Prom Dates idea."

But Penny shook her head. "I won't stand a chance."

"Defeatist!" Mike accused. "I'll vote for you."

"Then I won't get a complete white-washing," Penny said. She breathed a small, ecstatic sigh. Even if she hadn't a hope of being chosen queen, it was wonderfully flattering to be nominated.

Mike walked home with her and when they got there they lingered on the front walk, talking and laughing, as

Penny had seen Pam and some boy do so many times. In fact, they were still loitering there when Randy Kirkpatrick's convertible drew up at the curb and Pam called, "Hi, you two." She asked Mike then, her tone honeyed, "Were you looking for me?"

"Nope," Mike said cheerfully, as he and Penny moved toward the car, her hand tight in his.

Pam's surprised glance went from Mike's and Penny's clasped hands to Mike's face. She looked at Penny then and a slight frown marred the smoothness of her brow beneath the soft dark hair. "What's wrong with you two?"

"Right, you mean," Mike corrected.

"Penny, tell me!" Pam commanded. "Don't just stand there looking as if something wonderful's happened."

"They look pixilated to me," Randy chuckled.

"Mike asked me to the Prom." Penny smiled up at him.

"And she's one of the candidates for Prom Queen," Mike added, smiling down at Penny. He transferred his attention momentarily to Pam. "Does that sound wonderful enough to explain the way we look?"

"Penny, how swell!" The warmth of Pam's tone seemed to fool Randy and Mike completely. Only Penny detected a faintly hollow note in it.

"I asked Pam to the Prom," Randy confided wistfully to the world at large, "but she hasn't even told me whether she'd go yet."

"I said I was practically sure I would," Pam told him quickly.

"Penny makes up her mind faster," Mike informed Randy. "Or maybe it's just my irresistible charm."

During the raucous laughter that followed, Pam got out of the car.

"Give you a lift home?" Randy asked Mike.

"Sure," Mike said. He squeezed Penny's fingers in farewell. "Be seeing you."

The convertible zoomed off and Penny turned to face Pam. But Pam was already on her way into the house. "Of all the double-crosses!" she flung across her shoulder.

Penny hurried after her. Luckily Mother was busy with a customer and Gran was talking to someone on the phone, so no one delayed the twins. In the privacy of their bedroom, Penny denied hotly, "It was not a double-cross!"

"I'd like to know what else you'd call it!" Pam's eyes were blazing. "Going after Mike behind my back!"

"I didn't!" Penny felt anger to match Pam's rising within her. She had meant to be diplomatic, to try to make Pam understand. But if Pam wanted to be stinky about the situation, she could be stinky, too. She heard her own voice, as though it belonged to some total outsider, saying coolly, "It's not as if you owned Mike or any other boy. I guess he has a right to like me best if he wants to. He made up his own mind."

Pam's eyes widened in astonishment. Obviously, this was not the attitude she had expected in Penny. For a moment she was speechless. And Penny took advantage of that moment.

She said, "If you'll just listen and not go blowing your top, I'll tell you what happened." And she proceeded to do so. As she talked, she felt her own anger fading. Why should she be angry with Pam? Why should Pam be angry with her? She tried hard to make clear just what her relationship with Mike was. A friendship which had grown gradually to be something more than that. A warm liking equally shared. An understanding and congeniality of interest that had brought them closer and closer together.

Finally Pam asked, and she didn't sound so angry any more, just indignantly questioning, "But if you two were gone on each other, why didn't you warn me when I told you I was going after him? Why did you just let me go ahead?"

Penny knew then that it was Pam's pride that had been hurt, nothing deeper. And she was glad. She assured Pam, "I didn't know how Mike felt till today. I thought it was just me. Honestly, Pam, I figured he was pretending to ig· nore you, in order to get you interested again."

Pam said drily, "That made two of us who were mis· taken."

Penny nodded. She admitted then, "It's the most abso- lutely wonderful thing that ever happened to me, having Mike like me. And when I think of going to the Prom with him—" she broke off to smile at Pam mistily. "You don't really care, do you, with so many other boys to choose among?"

Suddenly Pam smiled, too. She reached out to give Penny a brief hard hug. "Not really, I guess. It's just that it's kind of startling to have you take a boy away from me. But, in a way, I'm glad it happened. You cer- tainly shouldn't lack confidence in yourself after this."

They laughed then, both of them, warm, healing laugh- ter. And it seemed to Penny that the closeness between them was a finer thing for the subtle shifting of values that had taken place. Always before she had felt that Pam contributed so much more to their relationship than she, Penny, ever could. Maybe some of the resentment she used to feel for Pam's greater popularity had grown out of her sense of inadequacy. But she didn't feel inadequate any more and her resentment was nothing but a wry memory. Now, in this moment, Penny felt secure at last in her own triumph as an individual. And Pam's manner seemed to be touched with a new respect, rather than the kindly pity Penny had sometimes sensed in her.

Being twins was going to be even more fun after this, she had a strong suspicion.

Chapter Twenty

SENIOR PROM

$\mathcal{T}$IME alternately flew and dragged during the next few weeks. Sometimes Penny thought that Prom night would never come. Then again it seemed she couldn't possibly squeeze in all the things she had to do before then.

"Relax," Mike kidded her. "You're so excited I'm afraid you're going to take off like a sky rocket."

Already their association had assumed a sort of form, or pattern. Mike came over to see her three or four nights a week. Sometimes they went out and sometimes they didn't, depending on their mood and the state of Mike's finances. But whether they did something special, like going in to Chicago to a show, or whether they just took a walk or sprawled in front of the record player, listening and talking and eating popcorn, both of them enjoyed it. The important thing was being together. There were so many things to talk about, so many interesting discoveries to be made about each other, how they thought and felt, what they planned to do with their lives. Mike, Penny learned, wanted to be a teacher.

"Maybe I'll never get rich," he grinned. "But it's a good life, with time for reading and writing, all the things I like to do. And I think it's an important job."

Penny thought so, too. She felt proud of Mike and

happy in the understanding that seemed to grow and deepen between them day by day.

During those crowded busy weeks, two surprising things happened. Mother got a quite overwhelming commission to do an extensive job of decoration at the country club. Which meant that Howard House was firmly established and Celia's professional reputation assured. It was Gran, however, who sprang the biggest surprise.

One evening at dinner, she announced out of a clear sky that she and Lucius Hancock had decided to get married. "It's only sensible," Gran said firmly. "We're very fond of each other and you'll be able to manage without me, now that the girls are practically grown up. And Lucius is so lonely, rattling around in that big house of his all by himself."

Mother, her eyes suspiciously bright, got up and went around the table to give Gran a hug and kiss. "Darling," she said, "we'll miss you dreadfully, but I think it's wonderful! I know you'll be happy. Lucius is a grand person."

Pam and Penny kissed Gran and wished her happiness, too. But when they were all seated again and the excitement had cooled down a bit, Pam looked at Penny and started to laugh. And Penny knew exactly what she was laughing at, so she got convulsed with mirth, too.

"What's wrong with you two?" Mother demanded, frowning.

And Gran looked quite huffy until Pam explained, between giggles, "It's just that we had Mother practically married to Paul and nothing came of that. But we didn't even dream that you and Lucius—" she dissolved into laughter once more.

But now they were all laughing together. It was a very

gay meal. And when Lucius came over later, the warmth and gayety continued. He seemed just like one of the family. But then, Penny realized, he had seemed that way for quite a long while, only they hadn't noticed it.

Finally it was only days till the Prom. Such full days, bubbling with such sweet excitement. The dance was to be held at the country club. Pam and Randy were double-dating with Penny and Mike. And afterwards the Kirkpatricks were turning their pine-paneled rumpus room over to their son and his guests. Randy had asked Pam and Penny to suggest all the people they'd like invited to his post-dance party. So it was to be quite a mixed crowd. Both the Headlines Club and Pep Club would be well represented. Penny was going to wear the lovely dress Gran had made for the Cupid Caper. And Gran had made Pam one just like it, only in yellow instead of green. But the off-shoulder necklines, the little stiff black lace peplums, were identical.

Never before had Penny looked forward to an evening with such anticipation. She had little hope of being chosen Prom Queen, but just to be one of the nominees, to have her friends in Headlines out campaigning for her, was a big thrill. It seemed to Penny that she had more friends than she had realized. So many people stopped her in the halls at school to wish her luck. This was due partly, she realized, to her work on Prom Dates. The bureau had matched up a considerable number of names. For the first time in school history, every senior girl who wanted to would be attending the big dance. And a lot of them figured they owed their chance to do so to Penny.

"You know," Maggie Wright told Penny one day as

they were walking home from school together, "you just might win."

Penny hooted derisively at the possibility. "With Pep Club backing Pam and Art Club solidly behind Laurie MacGregor? You mad dreamer!"

"Yes, but—" Maggie broke off with a little shrug. "Well, we'll see. I don't want to get your hopes up."

"Don't worry," Penny laughed. "You won't."

At last the magic night came. All day it had rained, but around dinner time the skies cleared and a sliver of new moon emerged from its curtain of clouds like a prima donna taking an encore. Such a flurry of activity overwhelmed the upper floor of Howard House that no one even knew about the moon till much later. After an early meal, partaken of in pin curls and frenzied excitement by the twins and in almost as great anticipation by Mother and Gran, the girls began getting ready. This involved a hectic succession of showers and manicures, of near-despair over a curl that wouldn't set right, a slip strap that broke at the last minute. But finally both Pam and Penny were ready. And it had only taken a little over two hours.

"You look wonderful, both of you," Mother told them, her eyes shining.

And Gran agreed, "They certainly do."

"You're just saying that," Penny teased, "because you made our dresses."

"Naturally," Gran nodded.

Mother laughed, collapsing on the couch beside Gran. "I'm certainly glad there aren't any more of you."

"So are we," Pam said, slipping her arm around Penny. "Two's company."

The doorbell sounded then and Pam begged, "Will you

let the boys in, Mother? We want to make an entrance."

As Celia went down the stairs, smiling, Pam and Penny rushed back into their bedroom. They giggled and whispered and fussed with their hair and make-up for a good ten minutes before emerging into the living room again.

Mike and Randy, who had been sitting on the couch, got to their feet hastily at sight of the twins.

"Wow!" Mike said, his blue eyes lighting.

And Randy said, "Likewise!"

Randy and Mike looked quite wonderful, too, Penny thought, in their white dinner jackets and black trousers. Especially Mike. He handed her a florists' box and Penny thanked him and took out the orchid it contained.

"Oh, Mike—it's beautiful," she murmured, her entranced gaze lifting from the lovely flower to Mike's face.

Pam was going through practically the same routine with Randy. Mother and Gran exclaimed admiringly over the corsages, too.

"We'll just carry them till we get there," Pam suggested sensibly. "Then we won't crush them with our coats."

"Good-bye, dears," Mother called after them as they went down the stairs. "Have fun, all of you."

"Don't expect us home till late," Randy warned her.

And Mother laughed, a reminiscent sort of laugh, and said, "I won't. It's Prom night."

After he had helped her into Randy's car and climbed in beside her, Mike whispered against Penny's cheek, "You'll really knock 'em for a loop tonight, baby. Am I a lucky guy!"

Penny thought, "I'm the one who's lucky," as she turned her lips for Mike's kiss.

The evening seemed to merge into a mad and lovely confusion, once they arrived at the club. The big ballroom was decorated in blue and gold, the school colors. The music was smooth as cream. Penny had enough partners to make her feel flattered and desirable. She danced with Mike and Randy and Bob Purcell. Then Mike again. She would just as soon have danced every dance with Mike, but, of course, she didn't tell him so.

Mike said, "Hi, beautiful," when he took her in his arms for that second dance. "Don't forget you're my girl."

"I won't," Penny murmured, feeling her heart bump happily under her pale green bodice.

Then it was time for intermission and a drum roll drew everyone's attention and silenced the babel. Through the microphone, the orchestra leader requested all the candidates for Prom Queen to please line up on the bandstand.

"Come on, Penny," Mike caught her hand excitedly.

He and Randy brought Penny and Pam to the foot of the steps. Together with the other nominees, the twins stood in the bright glare of the lights, smiling out over the circling crowd of faces.

"Isn't this fun?" Pam whispered, squeezing Penny's hand. "Aren't you popping?"

Penny could only nod. Even when the losers were winnowed out, she'd have this shining moment to remember.

Another roll of drums and the school principal, Mr. Weaver, looking unaccustomedly formal and handsome in his dinner jacket, stepped forward. In his plump hands was a crown of imitation jewels. "It is my great honor," he said portentously, "to bestow this crown on the girl, chosen by the vote of her classmates, to rule over tonight's festivities as queen. Also it will be my privilege to name the six girls who have been chosen by student vote to serve as her Court of Honor. But first—" Mr. Weaver's slightly unctious voice droned on and on and Penny let her eyes and her attention wander. Mr. Weaver never could resist the opportunity to make a speech. Her seeking glance found Mike, down there in the front of the crowd, and she smiled at him. And Mike beamed back proudly.

At last Mr. Weaver wound up his remarks, which had taken all of ten minutes. "And now," he said, "it gives me great pleasure to place this crown on the head of the most popular senior girl at Glen Township High." As he spoke, he was moving down the line of candidates toward Pam and Penny.

"Pam's going to get it," Penny thought, the tension of waiting building up unbearably within her.

Pam was feeling the tension, too, Penny realized, wincing slightly at the tight grip of Pam's fingers on hers under cover of the bouffant skirts of their dresses.

"Miss Penny Howard," Mr. Weaver said, quite unbelievably, so that Penny stared at him blankly for a moment, until she felt the slight pressure of the glittering crown as Mr. Weaver placed it on her head.

Then she knew that it was true. She had been chosen Prom Queen. Most popular senior. How it had happened, she couldn't imagine. But the weight of the crown on her head lent the absolute touch of reality.

After that there was applause, there was cheering. Pam hugged Penny and pressed her cheek tight against hers, not kissing her, for fear of smearing their lipstick, but exclaiming, "I'm so glad, Pen." If she was also surprised, or disappointed, she hid it well.

When the din had been quieted with another drum roll, the Court of Honor was named. Pam was among those.

So Penny hugged and congratulated her, too. And the losers descended the steps of the bandstand, smiling as if they didn't care.

All the rest of the intermission was filled with congratulations for the lucky winners, their friends clustering proudly about them. Penny's friends were the proudest of all, Maggie and Jean and Bob, so many, many others. More friends than Penny had known she had. And Mike, of course. Mike, standing there solid and smiling beside her, moving away only long enough for Penny to pose with her court for pictures to appear in the school annual, the *Crier*, the *Glenhurst Daily Journal*.

"Ah, fame," Mike cracked, slipping his arm through Penny's when the music finally began again. "Is it getting you down a little?"

Penny said, "It's wonderful—but—"

Pam, just behind her, put their feeling into words bluntly, "But, personally, I'd like to get off somewhere for a minute to catch my breath. You, too, Pen?"

Penny nodded. And Randy, whose arm was through Pam's, said, "I know just the spot. Follow me, chillen."

He led them down a hall to the trophy room, whose deep leather chairs and couches were inviting and deserted.

"Just the place," Pam murmured, collapsing onto a long couch. "Won't you all join me?"

The four of them sat down, side by side, deep on their spinal columns, their legs thrust out before them. Music filtered in faintly from the ballroom.

"Boy," Mike said, "this is something like!"

Randy put his arm around Pam and she leaned her head on his shoulder. Mike's arm went around Penny.

"Pardon me," he said with mock gravity, "but your crown's on crooked."

Penny laughed and, taking it off, set it on her lap. "I still don't know how I happened to get it," she admitted.

"Shall we tell her?" Mike asked the others.

"It might go to her head," Randy suggested.

"No, it wouldn't," Pam said. "Penny's not the type to get carried away because she's the most popular girl in the senior class."

"But I'm not," Penny said. "Not really. It was—well, maybe it was because of the date bureau."

"You see?" Pam said. "She's modest."

Their eyes met in a long, level look of understanding. And Penny thought what a change the year just past had made in their relationship. They were as close, or closer, than ever. But it was a closeness now of mutual respect, not of one leading and one following. No longer did she resent Pam, or envy her. There was no cause to. As for friends, she might not win them so easily as Pam, but she had as many. Tonight had proved that. Maybe, Penny thought, the fact that you had to work harder for the things you wanted to achieve wasn't such a disadvantage after all. Who minded a little work when the results were so imminently satisfactory?

Pam turned her attention back to Randy once more. Penny's glance fell on the crown on her knees. Its imitation jewels winked back at her. But she only stared at it for a minute, this tangible symbol of her achievement. Then her eyes lifted to Mike's.

"Hi, Queen," Mike said, his blue gaze reaching deep, his arm tightening about her.

"Hi," Penny murmured.

As Mike's lips came down to meet hers, the crown slipped off her lap and lay on the thick carpet. And Penny didn't even notice.